Dear Reader,

We have exciting news! Starting in January, the Harlequin Blaze books you know and love will be getting a brand-new look. And it's *hot!* Turn to the back of this book for a sneak peek....

But don't worry—nothing else about the Blaze books has changed. You'll still find those unforgettable love stories with intrepid heroines, hot, hunky heroes and a double dose of sizzle!

So be sure to check out our new supersexy covers. You'll find these newly packaged Blaze editions on the shelves December 18th, 2012, wherever you buy your books.

In the meantime, check out this month's red-hot reads.

LET IT SNOW by Leslie Kelly and Jennifer LaBrecque
(A Blazing Bedtime Stories Holiday Edition)

HIS FIRST NOELLE by Rhonda Nelson
(Men Out of Uniform)

ON A SNOWY CHRISTMAS NIGHT by Debbi Rawlins
(Made in Montana)

NICE & NAUGHTY by Tawny Weber

ALL I WANT FOR CHRISTMAS
by Lori Wilde, Kathleen O'Reilly and Candace Havens
(A Sizzling Yuletide Anthology)

HERS FOR THE HOLIDAYS by Samantha Hunter
(The Berringers)

Happy holidays!

Brenda Chin
Senior Editor
Harlequin Blaze

Tawny Weber

NICE & NAUGHTY

HARLEQUIN®
entertain, enrich, inspire™

Recycling programs
for this product may
not exist in your area.

ISBN-13: 978-0-373-79730-1

NICE & NAUGHTY

Copyright © 2012 by Tawny Weber

ABOUT THE AUTHOR

Tawny Weber has been writing sassy, sexy romances for Harlequin Blaze since her first book hit the shelves in 2007. A fan of Johnny Depp, cupcakes and color coordinating, Tawny spends a lot of her time shopping for cute shoes, scrapbooking and hanging out on Facebook. Come by and visit her on the web at www.tawnyweber.com.

Books by Tawny Weber

HARLEQUIN BLAZE

To get the inside scoop on Harlequin Blaze and its talented writers, be sure to check out blazeauthors.com.

To my very own Persephone,
who really does climb Christmas trees,
but never tears the heads off teddy bears.

1

"DUDE, I CAN'T BELIEVE your luck with women."

"That's not luck, my friend. That's an abundance of charm," Detective Diego Sandoval offered with a wicked grin. "And the simple fact that I love women."

And with a few painful exceptions, women loved him right back.

Something that came in handy when he was charming information, and a cast-iron frying pan, out of a three-hundred-pound mass of quivering fury.

"I've never seen anyone so pissed, though. When you arrested her old man, I thought she was gonna knock you on your butt. By the time you left, you had her ready to testify against the dirtbag, handing over evidence and offering to make you a bologna sandwich."

Diego shrugged. He was a cop. That was his job, his focus, his entire life. He did whatever it took to break a case. "Try chilling a woman down while she's aiming a sawed-off shotgun at your goods."

"Suspect?"

"Date."

Following Diego up the steps of the large brick building that housed the Central California Sheriff's Field Operations Bureau, Chris Carson shook his head. In admiration or in disdain, it didn't matter to Diego. He was all about the job and he devoted 100 percent to it. He didn't have time to worry about other people's opinions or doing the buddy thing. That's what made him one of the best.

"Someday, Sandoval, you're gonna meet a challenge you can't charm your way through," Chris said as they strode down the hall toward the patrol and investigation offices.

Diego's grin slipped a notch.

"Someday" had happened at birth. Diego had heard tell over the years about such a thing as motherly love, but he'd never experienced it himself. Hell, his mother had barely tolerated him. His learning to talk had been her breaking point. At three, he'd begun the loser shuffle between the rigid disapproval of his uncle Leon's house and the dismissive foster home's revolving door. Every couple of years, his mom would feel the guilt and haul him back. But those dance breaks never lasted.

No matter. That was then. Diego only cared about now.

"Most women don't need weapons," he told the younger man, leading the way through the bullpen. "Mother Nature made sure they were born armed and dangerous."

Before they reached Diego's desk, one of the other cops shouted his name.

"Captain called down a half hour ago, Sandoval. He wants to see you."

"Yeah?" Diego tossed his leather jacket over the back of his chair, then lifted the stack of file folders off the corner of his desk to find one that Chris had been looking for before they left earlier.

"Immediately."

The room chilled. Chris grimaced, glancing around for an escape route.

Diego flipped through folders anyway. He wasn't oblivious to the potential drama. He just didn't give a damn. The case was what mattered and he was sure he had one that tied in with the bust they'd just made. If Chris moved on it, they could nail this drug dealer for twice as long.

"I can get the file later," Chris muttered. "Kinnison hates waiting."

"He's waited a half hour. Two more minutes isn't going to matter."

The chill in the room turned antsy, nervous.

Diego kept right on flipping files. For a bunch of seasoned cops, these guys were way too intimidated by the new brass. Captain Kinnison had been on the job for three months, but it'd taken him only two weeks to institute a new order in the station house. An order heavy on rules, regulations and protocol. And politics. All things Diego didn't give a rat's ass about.

Something that hadn't earned him any points with his new boss. Despite that, though, word had come down two days before that he was up for a coveted transfer to the San Francisco Sheriff Department, complete with a promotion to Homicide.

For the most part, Diego was the cocky, lone wolf his uncle claimed him to be. One who didn't look for back pats, didn't see the promotion as a big deal. But a little, rarely acknowledged part of him was like a kid on Christmas who'd just found his secretly dreamed-of present under the tree—proof that while he might not be the favorite, Santa still thought he was on the right list.

The move to San Francisco was ideal. Fresno was getting claustrophobic, like the small towns Diego had hated when he was growing up. The promotion to Homicide validated everything he'd done, everything he was. And he was up for it because he was a damn good detective with the highest close rate in Fresno County. Not because of ass kissing and cronyism. Ironic that by insisting on doing things his way, he'd garnered a file full of commendations and a fast-track to big-deal promotion. He'd finally done something that disproved his uncle's and uptight cousins' assertion that he'd never amount to jack.

"Sandoval, in my office. Now."

The command was quiet. Intense. And seriously pissed.

"Good luck," Chris muttered, knocking a chair into Diego's desk in his rush to get away.

"Hey," Diego called before he could get too far. The deputy grimaced, shooting a quick glance over Diego's shoulder before taking the file folder he held out.

Diego tossed the rest of the stack on his desk, ignoring its precarious slide toward the edge. Then he turned to face the captain's stony stare.

"On my way, sir."

Diego had a brief vision of walking the plank toward a very large, very hungry shark. Then he shrugged it off. What was the worst the guy could do? Take a bite out of his ass? Diego stepped into the office. The captain, already seated behind his large desk, inclined his head toward the door. Shutting it behind him, Diego took a seat. Good. Ass bitings were always better done in private.

His face as hard as the oak of his desk, Kinnison didn't waste time with games.

"The D.A. has some issues with yet another of your cases, Detective Sandoval. Since we've had similar chats so often over the past few months, I'm sure you're aware of how much I dislike hearing that you didn't follow procedure. Again. By not playing by the rules, you've compromised the prosecutor's chances of getting a conviction. Again."

A dozen arguments ran through Diego's mind, but he clenched his jaw shut and waited.

"You threatened Geoffrey Leeds with—" the captain made a show of looking at the paper in front of him, even though they both knew he didn't need to "—an offer to wrap his large intestine around his throat and choke him with it."

"*Offer* being the operative word, sir," Diego pointed out. "I didn't threaten. I offered."

"And the difference is?"

"He could have said no. He didn't have to tell me the details of the porn ring he and his buddies were running in the high school gymnasium."

Captain Kinnison's stare could have made a polar bear shiver. Before the older man hauled out his lecture on se mantics—again—Diego inclined his head toward the file.

"Didn't the D.A. read the letter Leeds signed, stating that he was volunteering the information of his own free will?"

"He read it. But he feels, as do I, that the defendant might have signed under duress," Kinnison said, a small, tight smile puckering his thin lips. "Which puts yet another open-and-shut case in question, thanks to your methods, Detective."

Kinnison had no interest in hearing a defense, so Diego kept his mouth closed and waited.

The captain didn't make him wait long. He set the file down, then held up a letter. With the morning sun shining through the window behind Kinnison, the logo of the San Francisco Sheriff's Department was visible through the thin paper.

Diego tensed.

He'd seen enough of them to recognize a job assessment form.

"Detective Sandoval, you're up for a promotion and transfer."

Damn. Diego tried to tell himself that not getting the promotion wasn't a big deal. He wasn't looking for a ladder to climb. His ego didn't ride on outside kudos.

But, he acknowledged with an inner grimace, he wanted that job. Wanted the challenge of working Homicide. Wanted, intensely, to get the hell out from under Kinnison's watch. Wanted it all so bad he could taste the bitter disappointment as he watched it slide out of his grasp.

"You have a strong record with the department," Kinnison mused, running the letter through his manicured fingers in contemplation. "Your peers respect you. The commissioner feels that your close rate is high enough to offset the cases lost by your roughshod style and disregard for regulations. Captain Ferris in SF Homicide is willing to consider your promotion based on my recommendation."

"But?" There was always a but.

"But there are some issues. The first being that you're not a team player. Add to that your lack of respect for protocol, your inability to follow orders and the way you blithely dance all over procedure. I can't, in good conscience, give you a positive evaluation."

Fury and frustration churned in Diego's gut. It was one thing to lose a promotion because he wasn't good enough, wasn't smart enough or just didn't have what it took. But to lose out because he didn't dot his freaking i's and put tidy crosses on his t's? Screw that.

"So you're going to, what? Withhold recommendation?" The mental image of Diego's uncle, wearing the same smug, arrogant expression as the captain, flashed through his head. The old man had always said that Diego's rebellious attitude would be his downfall. Maybe he should drop him a note, let him know he was still right.

"No. Denying you recommendation might be appropriate in this situation, but it wouldn't serve me in the long term."

In other words, while Kinnison would love to screw him out of the promotion as a punishment, he'd given up on making Diego toe the line. So he'd rather get him out from under his command. He just wanted to mess with him before he did.

"Then what's the deal?" Diego asked, wondering how the guy was going to reconcile the two.

"You're going on special assignment."

And there it was. His punishment. And his last chance. That promotion was close enough to taste. And it tasted mighty sweet. But even more appealing was the chance to work under a different captain.

"What assignment, sir?"

"You'll be reporting to the mayor of Diablo Glen in the morning to investigate their little crime wave."

Diablo Glen. Tiny town, nestled in the foothills of Sequoia National Park. Too small to have its own police force, towns like that usually rented out a deputy now and then or had a low enough crime rate that they could rely on the occasional sheriff patrol.

"I don't do small towns," Diego stated, his throat tight. The truth was, he hated small towns. Close-knit, judgmental and unyielding. "My skills are better suited to cities. There isn't a whole lot of vice in the boonies."

"Oh, you'd be surprised." His smile about as friendly as a shark's, the Captain leaned forward to hand a file across the desk. Smelling a trap, Diego hesitated for a second before taking it.

"Diablo Glen has need of your services, Detective. This crime is right up your alley. It seems they have a series of rather odd burglaries."

"My specialty is vice, not burglary."

"The line is blurry in this case." The captain inclined his head again, this time toward the file.

Trapped, Diego opened it. Thirty seconds later, he shook his head. "No way. Absolutely not."

"You're refusing a direct order from a commanding officer, Detective?"

The older man didn't have to voice the threat. It hung there over their heads like a swinging blade, glinting right over Diego's neck. As much as he wanted Diego out from under his command, the guy would veto the promotion if he didn't get his way. Fury and frustration battled for supremacy in Diego's belly as he glared.

"I have no choice at all?"

"None," the captain verified with a smile as wide and satisfied as a cat in a fully stocked mouse house. "You are now assigned to the tiny little town of Diablo Glen until their mayor is satisfied that you've solved this case. And you will solve it by the book. No hotdogging, no skirting the system. To do so, you'll have to play nice with the locals. And you'll have to show the utmost respect for the department's rules and procedure."

Diego's jaw ached from the effort to hold back the furious rant. Finally, when he was sure he wouldn't spew swearwords and abuse, he inclined his head. "I'm going out on a limb here and guessing that my closing this case, your way, is mandatory if you're going to sign off on my promotion."

"Exactly, Detective. You want your promotion, you need to catch a panty thief."

2

"WHAT DO YOU THINK of a sheer peekaboo red nightie with white fur trim paired with over-the-knee patent boots?"

Cringing, Jade Carson shook her head so hard she almost dumped a whole spoonful of red sugar on cookie Santa's jolly face.

"I think those are three things that should never go together, Beryl," Jade told her younger sister decisively. "It's like mixing beer, chocolate truffles and mashed potatoes. They're all fine on their own, but together they're every kind of wrong."

"Ew," her eldest sister, Ruby, said in agreement.

"What's wrong with beer and mashed potatoes?" Beryl asked. "I mean, I wouldn't have the truffle at the same time, but maybe afterward for dessert?"

"Are you sure we're related?" Jade asked Beryl, shifting her focus from lining the chocolate jimmies around Santa's boots to peer at her sister.

A silly question.

Nobody peeking through the greenery-festooned garden window could take them as anything but siblings. Any of the Carson sisters could have graced the top of the Christmas tree, with their flaxen hair, wide green eyes and dimples. But when it came to personalities, they were as different as their hairstyles.

A CPA, Ruby was labeled the smart sister. Her hair was as practical as she was. She wore a sleek pageboy long enough to be pulled back for exercise or tax season, both of which she claimed kept her in prime shape. Beryl was deemed the sweet sister by the good people of Diablo Glen. Her blond curls waved to her shoulder blades. The romantic look, combined with her soft heart and slightly ditzy personality, gave her a fragile air.

The creative sister, Jade was neither practical nor fragile. Her hair was long, edgy and razor straight with low-swept bangs sassy enough to counteract her dimples. Her style was more rock-star than small-town, and she often said that her attitude was her best accessory.

"You are the one with the degree in fashion," Ruby pointed out, just this side of snickering. "Why don't you explain to her why the style doesn't work."

That was the thing about fashion, though. It was all subjective. What made one person feel fabulous would make another cringe, and yet another feel as if they were dressed in an alien costume. And though most people would cry foul over tennis shoes, a tank top and a tuxedo together, she'd seen it pulled off with panache. Fashion always depended on the person, and whether they had the attitude to pull the look off or not.

"Maybe I'm just a prude when it comes to my sisters," Jade muttered, shrugging away her odd discomfort. She, herself, didn't know why the idea of Beryl dressing as a slutty Santa for her fiancé was so cringeworthy. So there was no way she could explain it to her sisters.

"Right," Ruby agreed as she slid the spatula under a chocolate reindeer to transfer it from the baking sheet to the cooling rack. "Except you were the one who threw my lingerie-themed bridal shower four years ago. And you helped me get ready for my wedding night, remember?"

"Didn't Jade buy you that black satin merry widow with red lace trim?" Beryl asked.

"She did. She also showed me how to adjust it so my boobs looked their perky best," Ruby acknowledged. She wiggled her brows at Jade and tossed a melting chocolate chip into her mouth before adding, "Ross appreciated your artistry, by the way. Anytime you want to work your magic again, feel free."

Jade grinned.

"That is just so sweet," Beryl said with a happy sigh, licking peppermint frosting off her knuckle before rinsing the bowl in the wide country sink. "Four years married, and you and Ross are still all googly over each other."

"Googly and giddy," Jade agreed, just as thrilled as Beryl over that fact. She loved seeing that happy-ever-after was actually possible.

The sisters had lost their dad five years ago. Their mother, who was diagnosed soon afterward with multiple sclerosis, had taken his death really hard. As they did with everything, the girls had found a way to share the care of their mother while keeping her life as normal as possible. As Opal's MS progressed, Ruby had taken on her mother's finances and responsibility for the general upkeep of everything. Beryl chose a local college so she could live at home, always there to help with her mom's needs. And Jade, after her dreams of turning her fashion degree into an awesome, exciting career in a big city went kaput, had returned to Diablo Glen, moved into a cottage near the family home and taken a job at the library where Opal was head librarian.

"That's what I'll have with Neal," Beryl predicted. "Years and years of googliness."

Jade's smile dimmed. She didn't know why. Instead of commenting, she dropped her gaze to the tray of sugar cookies, as if messing up the decorations meant the end of Christmas as they knew it. There was nothing wrong with Neal. Maybe he was a little boring, and not quite the type Jade would have picked for her flighty sister. But he was a nice enough guy who earned a decent living and most of all, he treated Beryl like a princess.

A princess he planned to make his queen in the new year, and haul off to a castle of her own.

Beryl, like Ruby, would be married. Off living her own life. And like Ruby, who'd moved to Santa Clara for better job opportunities, Beryl would likely be fleeing the Diablo Glen nest, too. Neal was already talking about where he wanted to go. Leaving Jade trapped in this small town, with the full responsibility for their mother's care falling on her shoulders.

And on top of it all, Beryl would be getting regular sex.

Which was probably the part Jade was most jealous of.

And didn't that make her quite the ultra bitch. Horny ultra bitch, she corrected. A sad, sad combination.

"You need googliness too, Jade. But you're so picky," Beryl decided, her voice muffled because she had her head inside the refrigerator.

Jade frowned. Was that any better than horny ultra bitch? Instead of denying it, she made a humming sound that could be agreement. Or "Jingle Bells."

"Oh, I know," Beryl exclaimed excitedly. The younger woman bumped the fridge door shut with her hip, then set the batch of cream-cheese cookie dough on the counter for the next round of treats and gave an excited clap of her hands. "I'll have Neal set you up with someone. He's got a huge family, with people always in and out of their house. He has a whole slew of cousins visiting for the holidays, even. I'm sure he can find a great date for you. What do you think? Maybe we can double this weekend?"

"God, no!" Shock and horror sped through Jade's blood at equal speed. A blind date, set up by her little sister's boyfriend? Why not just force her to parade through town naked, wearing ugly discount-store shoes? That sounded a little more fun and much less humiliating.

"Why not? It'd be fun."

"I'm not interested in dating. And if I were, I definitely wouldn't need my little sister's boyfriend finding me a pity date."

"Fiancé, not boyfriend," Beryl corrected, smiling softly as she tilted her hand from side to side so the diamond glinted. "And you should be interested in dating. It's been four years since that jerk, Eric, ran off to join the circus. You've hardly dated, and when you did, nobody lasted more than a month. C'mon, Jade. Give it a chance."

Join the circus was her sisters' disdainful dismissal of Jade's fiancé ditching her at the altar to follow his dream of being a big-city attorney. She knew he figured he'd done her a favor by not making her choose between him and her responsibility to her family. So she tried not to be bitter.

But being a good sister—and hey, a girl's got the right to be a little bitter about losing her wedding night—she never bothered to correct their nasty comments about Eric. Why ruin the fun?

"Don't nag, Berry," Ruby chided as she arranged the last of three dozen chocolate-peppermint sandwiches in a decorated tin for the bake sale. "If Jade wanted to date, she would."

"Well, she's got to want sex," Beryl argued, giving Jade an arch look of inquiry. Unable to deny that she hated this long dry spell, Jade just shrugged. "Aha. See! So unless you're planning to call Horny-for-Hire, you have to do some dating to get to the sex."

"Horny-for-Hire?" Jade asked, laughing too hard to be offended. Besides, Beryl was right. She was a big fan of sex and seriously missed the opportunity to enjoy it on a regular basis. It just wasn't worth going through the dating drama to get it, though.

"You know what I mean."

"I know that you're a sweetie who wants everyone to have what you do," Jade said, truly appreciating that her sisters cared enough to want her as happy as they were. "But it's not that simple. Nor is it something I have the time—or the inclination—to deal with right now."

"Aren't you the one who's always saying that it's the everyday choices that count most? Or that there's no time like the present to get off your ass and fix your life? Or, you know whatever those other feel-good sayings are that you're always quoting from those empowerment classes you teach?"

"You're paraphrasing the message just a little, there." Jade grimaced. Still, Beryl was right. That was pretty much the message Jade included in all her presentations.

The classes had started out as a simple Dress for Career Success talk for teenagers that she'd offered at the library. Somehow midtalk, she'd sort of drifted from making an impression through clothes to why every woman deserved to pursue her dream career. Since Jade was currently working in a library—where, let's face it, fashion was closer to a word in the dictionary than an actual trend—she'd felt a bit like a fraud. But the kids—and many of the parents—had loved the presentation. So much so that the following month, she'd been asked to tweak the presentation for the ladies' club.

A year and a half later, Jade still felt like a fraud, but

her workshop repertoire had expanded from Fashion and Career Empowerment to Embracing Sexuality, The Art Of Saying No, and Lingerie for All Ages. Not too bad for a woman who wasn't living her dream career *or* getting any regular nookie.

Still, it was enough to make her want to dig into the bowl of chocolate chips for a little comfort.

"Isn't being empowered about creating a life that makes you happy?" Beryl prompted. "And for that, you need a man, of course."

Shocked, Jade dropped the chocolate morsels back in the bowl and stared. She couldn't have heard that right.

"Of course?" Ruby repeated, so offended her voice hit five different decibels. "Nobody needs a man to make them happy."

"They do if they want sex," Beryl countered with a gloating smile only a sheltered and slightly spoiled twenty-two-year-old could pull off.

Ruby and Jade exchanged eye rolls, but neither was willing to delve into the ins and outs of self-pleasuring during their baking marathon. But Jade made a mental note to add a Sexing Solo workshop to her spring-workshop offerings.

"Part of being empowered is being able to say no," she pointed out gently instead. "It's also empowering to accept someone else's decision with grace."

Beryl's lower lip poked out for a second as visions of fun double dates burst in her head. Then, in her usual cheerful fashion, she shrugged it off. "Fine. If you don't want to date, that's your call. So, where's the cookie press?"

Used to Beryl's verbal one-eighties and non sequiturs, they all scanned the kitchen. The three large green-and-red bins they'd hauled in that morning to start preparing for the Carson Holiday Open House were stacked against one wall. Held every year on the twenty-third, it was a little over two weeks away. Just enough time to make and bake every delicious holiday treat in Mom's cookbook. Jade sighed.

"We're missing one bin," Ruby realized. "It's probably still in the garage."

"I'll get it."

Jade waited until the kitchen door shut behind Beryl before shaking her head.

"A blind date," she breathed in dismay. "Seriously?"

"The mind boggles at the horror," Ruby agreed. Then she gave Jade a long, considering look. "She's right, though. You do need a date. Just not a blind one."

"I don't think so. In the first place, I have no interest in dating. In the second, even if I did have an interest, one of the joys of small towns is that there is nobody here to date. The men are all too young, too old, too married or just too icky."

"Not all of them," Ruby objected. "There are one or two nice single guys within your optimal age-dating range."

"Optimal age-dating range?" Jade repeated with a laugh.

"You know what I mean."

Sliding the tray of decorated cookies toward her sister and accepting a new one of raw shapes, Jade sighed. "Sure. Charlie Lake is home for the holidays and asked me out last week. Mark Dinson is managing the bank now and he's invited me to dinner a few times."

"But…?"

"But while they might be within the optimal dating-age range, and non-icky, they just don't do it for me." Jade gave a discontented shrug.

"You're not still holding on to—"

"No!" Jade interrupted, knowing exactly where her sister was going. "I'm not hung up on Eric. I'm not letting his leaving me at the altar affect my trust in the opposite sex.

And believe me, the sex with him wasn't so great that it ruined me against orgasms for life."

"How long's it been since you got lucky?" Ruby asked, not looking convinced, but obviously not wanting to argue.

Her last block of resistance crumbling, Jade scooped up a handful of mini milk chocolate chips and tossed a few in her mouth.

"It's been a while," she acknowledged, figuring that sounded better than admitting it'd been eighteen months, long enough to make her feel almost virginal. "But what are the options in Diablo Glen? I mean, it's not like I can just go up to one of these guys who live here and say, 'Hey, I'm not really attracted to you, you don't melt my panties and I don't want a future together. But d'you suppose you could scratch an itch for me?', now, can I?"

Coming over to sit at the table with Jade, Ruby pushed the sleeves of her red sweater up before carefully counting out twelve chocolate chips for herself.

"You know, most of the guys around here would probably go for that just fine."

"Which brings us back to icky," Jade pointed out.

Yet another reason to wish she lived in a big city. The anonymity offered so many sexual possibilities. Not that she was looking to turn her life into a series of one-night stands. But a chance to scratch an itch, a few delicious orgasms here and there, and the freedom of not having to see the guy again unless she actually wanted to?

That dream appealed to her almost as much as the dream of a career as a fashion stylist. Ever since she'd been old enough to dress her Barbies, she'd loved creating looks, putting together outfits and developing signature styles. By eight, she'd even taken her Ann doll from raggedy to bohemian with just a little tie-dye and tiny pair of faux-leather boots.

"Speaking of icky," Ruby said, finishing off her measly dozen morsels and getting to her feet as the timer dinged. "Did you hear the latest in the Panty Thief Caper?"

Jade wrinkled her nose. "There's nothing caperish about a creep who sneaks into women's bedrooms and steals their undies."

"Men's, too," Ruby said, setting a tray of cookies on the cooling rack and putting another in the oven. "I heard old Ben Zimmerman was having a fit. He won't say what was stolen, but he's still screaming up a storm."

"He's going to scream louder when his unmentionables end up paraded through town. This creep left the latest pair of panties hanging from the top of the cart corral at the grocery store this morning, along with a note that said 'No Peeking.'"

"What do you think it's all about?"

"It's a nuisance." Jade shrugged.

"That's it? A nuisance? Don't you worry, living alone like you do? How do you know your panties are safe?"

"Oh, please," Jade dismissed with a laugh. "Just a few minutes ago you were trying to get some guy into my panties."

"Don't joke, Jade. This might not seem like a big deal now, but you don't know what could happen. Someone this unstable could easily shift from stealing when people aren't home to sneaking in when they are. From taking panties from the dresser to tearing them right off women."

Jade wrinkled her nose. It was hard to be scared of something that screamed prank.

"I think you're reaching a little."

Ruby got that stubborn look on her face. The one that said she'd made up her mind and wouldn't let it go until she'd made up everyone else's, too.

"I hear that Mayor Applebaum is bringing in a detective to solve the case," Ruby added, her tone triumphant. As if that proved her right for worrying.

"A cop? For this?" Jade laughed. "And not for the pumpkin-smashing spree from a few months ago? Or the spate of dirty phone calls everyone was getting last summer? I mean, talk about sexual harassment."

"Or Persephone's holiday-property destruction binges?" Beryl said as she returned with another green bin.

"Hey, now," Jade chided with a laugh. "Leave my cat out of this."

"Well, you have to admit, she is a nuisance," Beryl pointed out, setting the bin on the floor by the others.

"But she only breaks into holiday displays and drags decorations around town," Ruby defended tightly, clearly upset that her sisters—who, unlike her, still lived in this town—weren't taking the situation seriously. "The pumpkins were tossed by kids on a dare. And those dirty phone calls, didn't someone trace them to an out-of-town number?"

"And this is someone with a panty fetish," Beryl said, laying out the cookie press and accessories. "No big deal. It's not like he's keeping them and doing pervy things."

"That we know of," Ruby snapped.

Beryl's chin lifted, her posture echoing Ruby's angry one. Time to change the subject.

"Let's switch jobs for a while," Jade suggested to Beryl, waving her hand toward the table full of deliciously tempting edible decorations. "I'll press spritz cookies, you dress Santa."

"You sure?" Beryl said with a frown as she glanced from the cookie disks she'd spread across the counter to the decorations. "You're usually so territorial about making the cookies look just right."

"Yep, I'm sure." She glanced at Ruby, then asked, "We

have two weeks until the open house. What else do you want to make today besides cookies?"

While her sisters debated fudge or pumpkin rolls, she filled the press. She needed the distraction. Not because she was worried about a creep with a panty fetish. But all this talk about panties, dating and sexual droughts was making her crazy.

If she wasn't careful, she'd start eating to numb the sexual frustration. She'd done that after Eric had left, putting on twenty pounds as she tried to deal with the emotional blow. For a girl who topped out at five-four, that'd been a quick wake-up call in how fast things could get out of control if she wasn't careful.

Still, it was a better option than finding herself a real Horny-for-Hire.

As Jade pressed out the first dozen starshaped cookies, she pretended they were flying across the sky and made a Christmas wish.

Please, let a sexy, gorgeous man sweep into her life just long enough to fulfill her every sexual fantasy. Give her enough good loving to last until she'd sorted out the rest of her life, then scooch on out without any hard feelings, leaving things simple and complication free.

And if she couldn't have the latter two parts of the wish, she'd settle on having a few of those sexual fantasies come true.

After all, she'd been a really good girl.

Wasn't it time she had a chance to be a little bad?

3

HER MIND FILLED with images of sexy guys all wrapped in bright red ribbons and nothing else, Jade strolled past the twinkling lights and animated Santa's workshop scene in Diablo Glen's version of winter wonderland, better known the rest of the year as Readers Park. One of the few perks of living in a small town was being able to walk everywhere. The library was only two blocks from her cottage, her mother's house a block to the east and the shopping district—if a dozen buildings could be considered a district—a block to the west.

The houses surrounding the park were dressed in their Christmas best, trees sparkling with festive decorations and eves strung with lights. Nobody did the holidays like people in a tight community.

But tonight, the quaint appeal and homespun warmth couldn't keep her attention. Jade couldn't get her sister's words out of her head. Was she only paying lip service to being empowered? Eighteen months was a really long time to go without sex. Well, it was if it was good sex. Maybe that was the problem. All the sex she'd had was pretty much mediocre. She scrunched her nose, remembering her ex-fiancé's fumbling fiver, as she'd nicknamed his lovemaking style.

She was only twenty-five. Too young to accept a sexless life. Not that she'd admit it to anyone—especially since it'd put a major dent in her tough, empowered image—but she wanted the kind of sex she read in those books so hot their covers were a blazing red. Just once, she wanted to experience that headlong rush of desire. To be overcome by passion. To need someone so badly, she could forget everything.

But unless star cookies had the power to make Christmas wishes come true, all that passion was going to stay between the pages of a book.

A little dejected and a lot frustrated, she crossed the street that ran between the park and her cottage. Left to her by her paternal grandmother, it was cozy, comfortable and cute. She'd just opened the latch on the white picket fence when a blur of black fur shot across her feet.

Yelping, Jade jumped back. Her book bag hit the ground, paperbacks sliding across the sidewalk like a colorful rainbow. Heart racing, she pressed her hand to her chest and tried to catch a breath.

"Persephone?" Jade's confused gaze slid from the now-smug cat pushing her way into the book bag to the front door of the cottage. It was closed tight. Glancing right, then left at the multipaned windows, she noted the sheers were still, indicating the windows were closed, too.

"How'd you get out?"

Thanks to her habit of viewing the neighbors' holiday decorations as enemies to be destroyed, Persephone was forced to be an indoor cat in December. Last week she'd escaped when Jade was hauling out the trash. Ten minutes later she'd found the cat batting foam presents at the tin soldiers on Mr. Turner's front lawn.

Kneeling to scoop books back into the cat-filled bag, Jade took a second to scratch Persephone's purring head. Brow furrowed, she craned her neck to get a glimpse of the side of the house. There, from her open bedroom window, fluttered a sheer white curtain.

"Uh-oh."

Her heart pounded so loud that her head throbbed with every beat. Forgetting the bag, the cat and books, Jade reached for her purse instead. Straightening slowly, she sucked in a shaky breath, telling herself there was nothing to be scared of. Yes, the town had experienced a rash of break-ins. But they were petty thefts. Not assaults. Despite Ruby's paranoia, there was nothing to be afraid of.

Still, she'd watched too many horror movies to be stupid enough to walk in there alone. With fingers that were only trembling a little bit, she fished her phone out of her purse.

It took her three tries to dial the mayor's office. It took the phone seven rings to go to voice mail.

"This is Jade Carson, and I think I've had a break-in. Can someone call me right back, please."

Applebaum was a hands-on kind of mayor, proud of always being available to the townspeople. His voice mail would forward to both his and his secretary's cell phones. Sure she'd hear back within five minutes, Jade took a deep breath and debated. She couldn't go inside. But that didn't mean she couldn't look around. Sweeping the books into her bag, she set it on the porch steps, but kept her purse— and cell phone— with her.

Careful not to step in the flower beds, she leaned forward to press her face to the living room window. Everything looked normal. Nothing to worry about, she assured herself as she continued around the side of the cottage. Her fingers curled around the windowpane, she shifted to the tiptoes of her four-inch-high boots. Squinting through the dusk-shadowed sheers, she peered into her bedroom.

And wanted to cry.

"Holy shit."

Jade would be the first to admit that she had a lingerie addiction. But seeing every piece she owned thrown around the room, tossed over the bed, dresser, floor and even the curtain rods, she wondered if she should look for a 12-step program.

Just as she was imagining herself standing in front of a bunch of strangers declaring her name Jade and confessing her love of tiny pieces of silk and lace, her phone rang.

"H'lo," she answered morosely.

"Jade, dear, this is Mrs. Clancy," greeted the mayor's secretary. "Are you okay? You think someone broke into your home?"

"Either that, or the Victoria's Secret Fairy had a tantrum in my bedroom."

"Oh, dear. The Panty Thief got you, too. Poor thing. You didn't go into the house, did you? You're not supposed to."

"No, ma'am. I'm looking through my bedroom window."

"Good, good. Mr. Applebaum is meeting that detective the sheriff sent. He's due anytime now. Not that I have much faith that he's any good. I overheard the mayor talking to the person in the county office. It sounded like the detective has some issues. And to be sent out here, on a case like this? Clearly that means he's bad at his job, right?"

Such a comforting thing to say to the most recent victim of the crime that the said detective had been sent to solve.

"Mrs. Clancy," Jade interrupted, leaning her forehead against the cool wood of the windowsill. She closed her eyes, but couldn't block out the image of her ransacked room.

"Did you hear they found another pair of underpants

this evening? Sheer, red with little pink roses sewn around the sides. Imagine that, sheer undies. I'll bet they were ordered from one of those catalogs. Not sure who they belong to, since the news hasn't traveled much yet. But someone will step forward, I'm sure. Panties like those didn't come cheap."

"Mrs. Clancy—"

"Not to worry, though. With a detective on the job, even if he's not a good one, I'll bet this is solved before your undies are left out in public somewhere. He should be here soon, too. I was making up a plate of cookies to take over. I imagine the young man is hungry after his long drive. And as he'll be staying at Mary Beck's bed-and-breakfast, you know he's not going to find anything good to eat there."

"Mrs. Clancy," Jade interrupted, louder this time. She blinked hard to clear the frustrated tears from her eyes, but couldn't push the feeling of angry embarrassment away as easily. "Please. Can you let the mayor know about my break-in now? It's getting chilly out, and Persephone is on the loose."

There was a loud gasp, then the sound of cookies tumbling and crumbling onto a plate. "There we go. Sugar cookies are just as good in pieces. I'll run this over right now, and the mayor will be there within ten minutes. You go catch that cat, Jade. If she gets into Carl's train one more time, he's going to be furious."

"Only if she eats the head off his teddy-bear ballerina again," Jade muttered to the dead phone. A new layer of nerves danced through her tummy. Thanks to some creep, her favorite pink silk thong was dangling off her vanity mirror. And now a strange, possibly incompetent cop was going to paw through her stuff.

And her cat, the scourge of Christmas decorations everywhere, was on the loose.

With a grimace and one more pained glance through the window, Jade turned, calling, "Persephone?"

So frustrated she was ready to cry, Jade made her way to her postage-stamp-size front porch, still calling for her pet. Usually the cat responded instantly. But Persephone wasn't stupid. She knew the minute she got within grabbing distance, Jade would lock her in the house.

Then she saw her across the street. Right on top of Carl's six-foot inflatable Santa snow globe. Jade squinted, then moaned. Yep. That was a teddy-bear head dangling from the black furry mouth.

DOUBLE-CHECKING the address, Diego parked his Harley in front of a two-story house that looked as if it'd been puked on by Christmas. Santa waved from a sleigh on the roof, danced with an elf on the lawn and flashed in lights, Vegas style, from the front porch.

This was the mayor's house? Why couldn't they have met at his office? This was so…small-town. Diego sighed. He wrenched his helmet off and scanned the view with a grimace. A tree glittered holiday cheer from the front bay window, and a beribboned pail of candy canes hung off the mailbox, inviting people to share one.

But it wasn't the effusive ode to holiday cheer that had him massaging his temple.

It was the man, probably in his sixties, romping around on the lawn while three kids clung to his back as if he was a bucking bronco. Or—Diego squinted at the brown sticks tied to the guy's head—maybe a flying reindeer?

Kinnison really knew how to twist the knife, shipping Diego off to a modern-day Mayberry. Small towns were worse than a gang-run ghetto when it came to trying to solve a crime. The residents banded together like glue, protecting their own. And while the ghettos had drugs, guns and prostitution, small towns had closed minds, uptight attitudes and suspicion of outsiders. And mayors who saw their citizens as beloved children to be protected.

It took all Diego's resolve to swing his leg over the bike and step onto the sidewalk. His tension didn't shift any when the older guy pulled out a friendly smile instead of a gun.

"Well, hello, there," the man said from his prone position, looking none the worse for wear as a fourth kid came barreling around the corner to latch onto the guy's neck like a demented squirrel monkey. "Can I help you?"

"I'm looking for Mayor Applebaum."

"That'd be me."

Of course it would. Diego didn't bother to sigh.

"Sir, I'm Detective Sandoval with the Central California Sheriff's Department."

"Ah." The mayor nodded, then with a few tickles, a hug or two and a direction to head on home for cookies, he dispersed the children and got to his feet. He watched them scurry over his lawn and up the steps of the house next door before giving Diego his full attention.

As long and lanky as he was graying, the man towered over Diego's own six feet. Brushing grass off his ancient corduroys, he came forward and offered his hand.

"Welcome to Diablo Glen." He gestured toward the matching detached garage next to the house, just as nauseatingly decorated as the house. "My office is in the town hall, of course, but I seem to get more work done here at home. Less interruptions, I suppose. Come in, we'll talk."

On edge, Diego followed.

"Kinnison sent you, then?" the mayor asked, opening the unlocked door. Following him in, Diego felt his shoulders relax for the first time since he'd got his new orders that afternoon.

Despite once being a garage, and the outside decor, this place was all business. The desk might be polished oak and the law books on the shelves leather, but it wasn't intimidating. Diego grinned at the life-size oil painting of the Three Stooges as he took the seat the older man indicated.

"Nice office," he said. This wasn't going to be so bad, he decided. He hadn't been looking forward to dealing with another micromanaging tightass like Kinnison, but this old guy seemed pretty chill.

Eyes twinkling, the mayor nodded his thanks as he took his own seat behind the large desk. As if just realizing he had it on, he pulled the reindeer-antler hat off and tossed it on the desk.

"I didn't get word who Kinnison was sending until an hour ago, which means all I have to go on is his assessment and a cursory check of your record." Before Diego could do more than frown, the mayor continued. "Kinnison would see a case like ours as an irritant. So I figure this goes one of two ways. Either you have a lot of potential, but somehow got on his bad side so he sent you here as a warning. Or you're too good to fire, but you regularly piss him off and he's trying to break you."

"You know the captain pretty well?" Diego sidestepped.

"We've served on a few of the same boards."

It didn't take years as a detective to read his tone and realize the mayor wasn't a fan of the new captain. Score one for the old guy's good taste.

All traces of teddy bear gone now, Applebaum tapped a finger on the stack of files on the corner of his desk. "Punishment, lesson or hand slap aside, I don't care that this sounds like a joke of a case. I expect it to be handled with tact, delicacy and a tenacious resolve for justice."

Kinnison's threats echoing through Diego's mind, he debated for all of three seconds. Then, unable to do otherwise, he opted for the truth. "I can only guarantee one of the three, sir. I've got the highest close rate in the county. I'm a damn good cop."

"But?"

"But I failed the course in tact, and have no idea what delicacy is when it comes to solving crimes."

"Then we might have a problem. This case involves a number of women, all embarrassed over the violation of their privacy. You're a stranger, a man, and a good-looking one at that. To solve this case, you're going to have to get them to talk to you about their unmentionables."

Diego grimaced.

Kinnison was probably laughing his ass off.

"I'll work on the tact, sir."

Applebaum's bushy brows rose, but he didn't mention delicacy again. He gave Diego a long, searching look. The same kind his uncle had always wielded, the kind that poked into the corners of a guy's soul. Uncle Leon had always come up disgusted after his searches.

Diego wondered how he'd convince Kinnison that being kicked to the curb before he even started the case wasn't the same as failing to solve it.

Before he could figure anything out, though, the mayor reached across his rosewood desk and lifted a thick file. Frowning, Diego took it without looking. His eyes were locked on the older man instead. What? No lecture? No warning about not causing trouble in his town?

"Well, then, let's see what you can do. Here are my files. They're probably a great deal more detailed than the ones you've seen. You go ahead and look through these, then we'll get to work."

We? Diego shifted. He didn't do partners. Especially not ones who saw the townspeople as friends instead of potential suspects. Still, the sooner he started, the sooner he could get the hell out of here. Small towns made Diego claustrophobic. Punishment cases just pissed him off. Not a good long-term combination.

"I'm ready to get to work, but I have a request first."

"You need a dictionary to look up the word *delicate?*"

Diego smirked. It was hard not to like a guy who'd honed his smart-ass mouth to such a sharp edge. "I realize this is your town, and your focus is on protecting your citizens. But I'd like permission to handle the case my way."

Eyes narrowed, Applebaum leaned back in his chair and studied Diego over steepled fingers. "Your way. Which means what, exactly?"

"I'll follow procedure, stick with the rules and regulations." Even if it choked him. "But I prefer to work a case alone. It's easier to form an unbiased opinion, to dig for and sift through information solo. I'm not asking you to stay completely out of it or to give me free rein. It'd just be easier if the victims, the townspeople, see me as the lead on the case."

"You don't want me breathing over your shoulder while you grill one of the ladies of my town about her underwear?"

Diego hesitated. Nothing said he had to let Applebaum ride shotgun. But edging him out could be seen as smudging that line the captain was crazy about.

Diego shoved a hand through his hair, noting that he'd forgotten Kinnison's order to get it cut.

Before he could address the tact Applebaum had mentioned, the door flew open. Surprised, both men watched a plump woman in a red Rudolph sweater hurry in, a plate in one hand and a sticky note in the other.

"I'm so sorry to interrupt. I brought cookies, but they're a little, well…" She set the red-and-white-striped plate on the desk so fast, at least a cookie's worth of crumbs hit the floor. Ignoring them, the woman hurried around the desk to hand the mayor the sticky note. Since she looked like the kind who chased crumbs like they were minions of the devil, Diego figured that note was damn important.

The frown on Applebaum's face confirmed it.

"Thank you, Clara," he said. Brow furrowed, he gestured to Diego. "Clara, this is Detective Sandoval. Detective, my secretary, Clara Clancy."

"Nice to meet you, ma'am."

"Likewise," she said with a quick smile before poking her finger at the note again. "You should go now. Jade can't enter her house until you get there, and Persephone's out."

The mayor rose quickly. He grabbed a couple of cookie pieces off the plate and gestured Diego toward the door. "You can read the files this evening. For now, we have another theft."

"Sir?" He did a quick replay of the conversation. "What's the significance of this burglary? Who is in danger?"

As he always did before approaching a volatile crime scene, Diego did an automatic weapon check. Surprised at how quick the older man moved, Diego lengthened his stride.

"Jade Carson is our librarian," the mayor said, hurrying around the back of the garage-slash-office. Diego was just about to point out that he preferred to use his own transportation and that his GPS was perfectly capable of finding the address.

Then they reached the carport and his mouth was too busy drooling to get the words out.

"Climb in," the older man said, sliding into the driver's side of the cherry-red '66 Corvette. "And buckle up."

Diego didn't see it as capitulation to follow orders. It was more like expedience. And—he breathed deep the smell of rich leather—appreciation.

"Sir, is there a reason why the current victim being the librarian necessitates the rush?" Noting the sheepish look on the mayor's face, why did he feel as if he was getting the runaround? In fine style, he acknowledged as the powerful roar of the engine kicked to life. But style or not, he didn't go into a scene blind. It wasn't a violent crime, the victim hadn't entered the premises. So what was going on?

"We're hurrying because, well, because of something that has nothing to do with the crime but a lot to do with keeping the peace." Applebaum's words were as tight and controlled as his hands on the steering wheel.

Diego sighed. Adrenaline, so high and intense a second ago, started dissipating. "Is this one of those small-town things?"

Applebaum gave him a look that was part warning, part amusement. "Jade's cat got out. That's how she knew someone had been in her house. The cat is likely causing trouble, so while you investigate, I'll be rounding it up, assessing the damage and pacifying the neighbors."

Applebaum parked the car, then gestured to the cozy-looking cottage. Slate-gray with soft pink trim, it looked like something out of a fairy tale. Diego's gaze scanned the neighboring houses. A crowd had gathered across the street in front of one lit so bright, it dimmed the stars. Squinting, he could make out a pair of feet dangling from the roof. Part of the decorations?

"This is it," Applebaum stated. "You go on in, do your job. I'll send Jade in after a few minutes."

Diego's eyes followed when the mayor gestured to the crowd. Only one looked to be a woman. Older, plump and wrapped in a bright pink tracksuit. The librarian?

"I'd solve this as soon as possible, Detective," the mayor said as they both exited the car. Frowning, he glanced at the crowd again. "People deserve to enjoy their holiday without this kind of thing hanging overhead."

"I'll do my best, sir. I'm hoping to have the case resolved before the weekend, and leave you and the town to your holiday celebrations in peace."

Diego glanced at the crowd again and shook his head. Yep, the sooner he got himself back to the safe anonymity of a city, the sooner he could celebrate the holidays the way he always did—by ignoring them.

4

CROUCHED ON CARL'S SHINGLED ROOF, the heels of her favorite boots digging into her butt, Jade shoved a frustrated hand through her hair, pushing it from a sassy tousle to a freaked-out mess. Fitting. After all, she was on a damn roof.

"Mayor Applebaum," she said to the man at the top of the ladder, trying to sound grateful instead of hysterical. "I appreciate your help, but I don't think you should be climbing on a roof to get my cat. Persephone is my responsibility."

And the mayor was pushing sixty. If one of them was going to fall two stories and land on Carl's nativity scene with a splat, it should be her. Younger bones healed faster.

"You didn't let her out, Jade. A burglar did, so nobody is going to blame you for her escape." When Jade snorted, the mayor sighed. "I'll deal with Carl. You go deal with the unfortunate reason the cat's AWOL."

Jade eyed the furious mountain of a man pacing the lawn below, his beefy arms waving in the air. In one hand was a headless, tutu-wearing teddy bear. In the other, a very large, very flat sheet of plastic that had once been a blow-up globe. Which was worse? Facing the devastation of her bedroom, or facing the fury that was Carl?

She glanced at the top of the roof where her bratty cat perched, a teddy-bear head still dangling from the black furry mouth. Maybe she'd just wait here for a while.

"Come on," the mayor ordered. "Detective Sandoval is already on the scene."

"Aren't you coming?"

"Nope. The detective would like to run this on his own. I'll lure Persephone in with Clara's sugar cookies. Then after I've pacified Carl, I'll bring the cat and see how our fine detective is holding up."

She followed him down the ladder, grateful when he planted himself between her and the still-shouting Carl. Avoiding her neighbor's eyes, she gave a guilty wave and scampered across the street. As she approached her front door, she pressed one hand against her churning stomach. She really shouldn't have taste-tested so many cookies.

She'd seen how trashed her bedroom was through the window. Nobody else hit by the Panty Thief had mentioned their undies being tossed around. Was this an actual burglary instead? And why was the mayor worried about how the detective would hold up? Was he as bad as Mrs. Clancy thought he'd be?

Knowing she was stalling, she took a deep breath. For the first time in her life, Jade had to force herself to cross the threshold of the tiny cottage, her feet dragging across the polished wood floors. She could hear movement at the end of the hallway, indicating that the cop was already back there.

Maybe she could wait here for him? She could call her sisters over for moral—and housekeeping—support before she had to face the destruction of her bedroom. Her fingers inched toward the cell phone in her pocket. The temptation was so appealing. But so was the voice in her head, clucking like a chicken.

Get a grip, she ordered herself. Tossing her black leather duster over the back of a chair, Jade tugged her tunic smooth over her hips, rubbed a scuff off the toe of her boot, then headed down the hallway.

Chin high, she stepped into her bedroom. And for the second time that evening, froze solid.

Only this time the reason had nothing to do with fear.

Nope, this was lust. Pure, sticky lust.

It was like a million sweaty, hot dreams. The kind that woke her in the middle of the night, aching with need and frustration. He stood in front of her dresser, one hand filled with little scraps of nothings she called underwear.

Intense need swirled through her. Her legs were like jelly, her stomach clenched with an edgy sort of desire. The kind that made her thighs tremble and her nipples tighten against her silk bra.

A bra, she realized, that matched the hot-pink panties dangling from his index finger.

Her breath knotted in her throat, Jade tried to clear her head. Her home, her undies, had been violated. But her brain was busy stripping the man naked. And from the look of him, naked would suit him just fine.

He was gorgeous. At least, he was from the backside.

She took a visual inventory. Tall, an inch or so over six foot. Broad-shouldered and slim-hipped with a butt so tight and hard her mouth watered. Arrow-straight black hair covered his collar and invited her fingers to test the weight of those strands to see if they were as soft and silky as they looked.

Then he turned, just his head, and met her gaze.

Heat poured through Jade so fast, she swore she had a

tiny orgasm standing there in front of a complete stranger with his hands in her panties.

His eyes were like midnight. Dark, intense and searching. As if he could see all the way into her deepest fantasies and clue in to her every secret. Nerves, the kind she'd never felt around a man before, assailed her. Jade bit her lip, trying to figure out what it was about him that was so enthralling.

"Can I help you?" he said. His voice was as sexy as the rest of him. Deep and throaty, with just a hint of a Hispanic accent. The kind of voice made for sexy pillow talk.

"Ma'am?" It wasn't the verbal nudge that yanked her out of the sexual stupor. It was the amusement in his tone that told her that he was not only aware of her overwhelming interest, he thought it was funny.

Nothing like being laughed at to clear a girl's head.

He turned to fully face her, offering the perfect view of his wide, sculpted chest hugged lovingly by a black T-shirt. Trying to ignore this new enticement, she kept her gaze on his amused face. Big mistake. Chiseled cheekbones, a full bottom lip made for nibbling and eyes so deep and dark she knew if she fell in she'd never climb back out. Her heart, already racing, tripped over itself.

"This is a crime scene. I'm going to have to ask you to leave until I speak with Miss Carson." His smile was a grin now, just this side of mocking.

"I'm Jade Carson," she said stiffly, stepping farther into the room. Her foot caught one of the pieces of fabric strewn over the floor, sending a black lace demibra across the hardwood, just inches from his motorcycle boot.

Her face burned as red as the silk panties dangling from her vanity mirror.

His smile faded. His gaze traveled from the small notepad in his hand to the black lace bra on his toe, then back to her.

"You're Jade Carson? The owner of this house, and—" his finger swirled to indicate the room "—all of this lingerie?"

"Yes." What? She might not have the overblown curves of a centerfold, but she looked damn good in her unmentionables. Maybe she could yank down her jeans and show him the dove-gray lace of her thong.

"You're the librarian?" he asked slowly. His gaze took a slow stroll over her body, his expression making her tingle with both nerves and desire. Those dark eyes met hers again, the look in them hot and intense before he shuttered his gaze.

Jade shivered a little, missing the heat and wondering what'd turned it off. And what it would take to turn it back on. After all, he'd already seen all her underwear.

"I'm Detective Sandoval," he said, that whisky-smooth voice official and just a little stiff. Like he'd just swallowed a rule book. "I'm investigating the Panty Thief burglaries."

Jade's gaze swept the room before she gestured with her chin to his little cop notebook. "No kidding?"

His lips twitched. But he didn't drop the official routine. Jade arched a brow. A man both sexy *and* disciplined? The mind boggled at the possibilities that combination inspired on a fantasy level. Throw in endurance and attention to detail and he was a dream come true. Or at least inspiration to come.

"Ma'am?" he prompted, frowning as if he was trying to figure out where her mind had wandered. She'd be glad to tell him. "I'd like to ask you a few questions, if that's okay."

"Sure." Even though she doubted any of those questions would involve dinner, dancing or a bottle of wine, her stomach still swirled in anticipation.

"Given the state of the rest of your home, I figure it's safe to assume your room didn't look like this when you left it. Can you tell me what time you left the house today and how much of this disorder is due to the break-in?"

"Since I had to be at the library at ten, I left around nine so I had time to stop at my mother's, then at the bakery to get pastries for the ladies' club. They hold their meetings at the library and we like to provide a snack for them."

And while she'd been out doing those regular-life things, someone had invaded her home and wreaked havoc.

Jade finally looked, really looked, at her bedroom. Her sanctuary.

Unlike rumors of the other thefts, which were simple cases of an underwear drawer being dumped on the floor and a pair of panties taken, Jade's room was trashed. Lingerie strewn about like confetti after a drunken bachelor party, her possessions knocked over, books not only thrown from the shelves but ripped in half.

Who the hell ripped up books? Forgetting that she shouldn't touch anything, she knelt down to gingerly lift the ravaged pages she immediately recognized as *Madame Bovary*.

This was a complete and utter nightmare. Swallowing hard as the full impact hit her, she straightened and pressed one hand against her churning gut, trying to see through the swirling black fogging her vision.

"It's not that bad," he said. He didn't sound distant anymore. Instead, his voice was soothing and mellow, almost friendly. She wished he'd stuck with the uptight tone.

"Compared to what?" she asked, furious at the tears clogging her throat. She didn't cry. Tears were useless, stupid. Even angry tears.

"Compared to what my place would look like if someone did this," he said, his words teasing. "Car magazines ripped apart, boxers dangling from the lamp. A Speedo hanging in the window for all to see."

His mock shudder made her laugh.

"Speedo?" Her now-clear gaze skimmed his body, from the T-shirt tight over hard, flat abs down his narrow hips. For just a second, she let her eyes rest on his zipper, imagining what he looked like in a teeny-tiny piece of spandex. She grinned, somehow sure he could make the fashion faux pas sexy.

"Really?"

"A gag gift from the guys at the station house. These thieves have no respect for quality, low or high."

Her eyes soft with appreciation for how easily he'd pulled her back from the edge of hysteria, Jade nodded. Well, well. Looked like Hottie Cop was more than just a gorgeous face and rock-hard body. Which qualified him as the hottest fantasy material she'd ever encountered.

An empowered woman would go for it, right?

Nerves danced the cha-cha in her stomach. She wanted hot sex. She wanted a fling. And she was empowered, dammit. But could she actually chase a perfect stranger with the intention of getting him naked?

It was as if Santa had heard her wish, decided she'd been such a good girl that she deserved a chance to try her hand at being really, really bad. But only if she was brave enough to play.

She wanted to be brave. She really did. But as she told the girls in her workshops, some things you had to work up to. Small, consistent steps. She swallowed hard, looking around the mess. Maybe she should clean up her underwear first. Then she could work on being brave.

DIEGO'D FIGURED that life's little ironies were what kept things interesting. Or provided the best torture. It was always a toss-up which was which. Letting his gaze cruise over the woman in the doorway, he figured this was proof yet again. Without the intense four-inch studded boots, maybe five feet and four inches could be measured between her toes and the top of her pale blond head. Mussed and a little wild, her hair looked as if she'd shoved her hands through it a few times, letting the bangs flop down in a long sweep over her eye and down to her shoulders. Sharp, angled features, huge green eyes and lips made to give a man sweaty dreams rounded out the fairylike looks.

Her body was a series of slender lines and soft curves. Legs nice enough to make his mouth water were tucked into boots that had enough edge to assure him that, despite her sweet face, she and the plethora of seductive lingerie were, indeed, well suited.

"I know it's difficult to tell, given the state of the room," he said, trying to bring his focus back to the case instead of wondering how it'd feel to have her wrap those gorgeous legs of hers around his waist. Or better yet, over his shoulders. Diego closed his eyes for a second, trying to find control. Kinnison, he reminded himself, letting the name work like a cold shower. "But can you tell if anything's missing?"

"Not without going through it all," she said. She took a deep breath, her breasts pressing against the heavy weight of that purple sweater and making his palms itch. "Can I touch anything?"

A list of possibilities, all better fondled while naked, flashed through his mind. Diego blinked twice trying to clear the deliciously tempting images away.

"Yeah, sure. Just touch the fabric, though. I need to dust the hard surfaces for prints. But I'll wait until you get your delicates picked up."

Diego slid the black silk he'd picked up earlier between his fingers, luxuriating in the softness. He'd bet the blonde's skin was even smoother, softer.

Suddenly the crappy assignment took on a tempting sort of appeal. The kind of appeal that was likely to get him in trouble. Because he was pretty sure charming a victim into bed was on the Don't list in Kinnison's rulebook.

Still…

"Nice panties," Diego said with a smile as lethal as the weapon strapped to his side. "I'm impressed."

"Yeah?" Kneeling on the floor to scoop up an armful, she gave him a teasing look from beneath lush lashes. "You're impressed by my underwear?"

"The quantity is a little awe-inspiring," he said, sidestepping the truth—and his interest—by keeping his words cool and distant.

A tiny frown creased her brow, as if she was disappointed he hadn't taken the flirtation bait. Then she focused on her lingerie again. And growled. The sound was low and sexy. The kind of sound a woman might make during sex. Wild sex. Wild, mind-blowing, "do it two more times to see if it was really that good," sex. Good thing this was a temp assignment and an easy case to wrap up. Because he was pretty sure this was a woman who could actually make him whimper.

"What kind of lowlife dirtbag treats silk this way?" the blonde muttered, cussing under her breath as she held a teeny-tiny pink leopard-print nightie. "What's the deal? I thought this creep was all about stealing panties. Why would he mess with my nightgowns?"

Forcing his attention away from the curve of her ass as she bent over to scoop armfuls of cotton nighties and sleep shorts, Diego considered the question. It was a good one, the same he'd been wondering himself when she'd walked in.

"Were they in the same drawer?" Unless her drawer was the size of a closet, he already knew the answer was no.

"I keep my lingerie in the armoire, my nighties and pajamas are in the chest of drawers."

Diego frowned, noting the two pieces of furniture she'd indicated were on separate walls. It'd be easy to assume the destruction was the result of frustration from not finding her panties right off. But it felt like more. This felt personal.

"We're probably dealing with a kid or some perv with an underwear fetish," he mused, rocking back on his heels. That'd been his—and the deputies' who'd written the previous reports—assumption of the case. But he'd learned years ago to listen to his gut over assumptions, his or anyone else's. "You don't have much in common with the other victims, though."

"You don't think so?" Dumping her armload of delicates into a laundry basket at the foot of her bed, she gave him an amused look with those cat eyes. "I don't know about that. We're all female. We all live in the same town. We all wear underwear. Well, there is the rumor floating around this evening that Ben Zimmerman had his undies snatched, too. Now, Ben does have a habit of dressing up as Little Bo Peep for Halloween, and I avoid hoopskirts like the plague. But other than that, I'd say we all have quite a bit in common."

Diego'd always had a hell of a time resisting a woman with a smart mouth. He eyed the white eyelet bedspread and collection of hardback books lining the shelves on either side of the curved iron bed. The shelf filled with family photos was untouched, other than a leopard-print bra dangling from one frame. Despite the abundance of sexy underwear, he hadn't come across a single sex toy. And given the feel of the scene, if there'd been one to be found, the culprit would have tossed it in the mix.

Diego glanced back at the petite blonde, looking like an irate fairy as she plucked her lingerie from furniture, curtain rods and shelves where it hung like the fruits of temptation.

She was hot. No question about it.

And he'd seen the look in her eyes. Sexual speculation, mixed with a whole lot of lust. He figured it was close enough to an invitation to move on, even if she had snatched it back pretty damn quick.

Except for two things.

One, she was on the other side of that hard line Kinnison had warned him not to cross.

And two, despite her lusty looks and fabulous taste in what she wore against her skin, she was obviously a nice girl.

And while he might risk Kinnison's wrath on the first, he never risked the heartbreak that came with messing with the second.

Still…

"You got a boyfriend?"

"Why, Detective, is the sight of my lingerie tempting you?" she teased, her tone flirtatious and light. But he saw that look in her eyes again. The "wouldn't it be interesting to strip you naked and climb all over your body" look.

Was she trying to kill him? Diego hadn't been this uncomfortably hard since he'd found a crack in the dressing room wall of the local strip club back when he was a teenager.

"Mixing business and pleasure is against regulations." And right now, he figured those regulations—and the promotion riding on them—were the only things keeping him from trying to find out just how nice a girl she was. He cleared his throat. "In cases like this, a boyfriend, an ex or a rejected admirer all fit the bill for crimes of this nature."

He couldn't help but grin when she ducked her head. Skin that fair sure blushed easily. There. Temptation handled. Now she'd think twice about flirting. Nice girls were easy to handle, he decided.

"No boyfriend, no ex, no rejected admirer," she told him, her words a little tense. Embarrassment? Then she met his eyes again. His brows shot up. Nope, that wasn't shyness in the green depths. It was irritation. Did the fairy have a temper?

"I hope you have more to go on than that to solve this case," she said, separating the clothing she'd gathered into tidy piles on her bed. Panties in this one, nighties in that. Diego swore a drop of sweat ran down his temple when a sheer red thong missed its pile and landed on her pillow. "Then again, rumor has it you might have a few problems with that."

So she could bite back. When had temper become sexy? Maybe when temper had such great taste in lingerie. Eyeing the tiny roses decorating the red thong, he asked, "Problems with what?"

"Solving the case."

Diego's gaze snapped to hers. "What are you talking about?"

Jade tilted her head to one side. The light caught on the row of tiny gold hoops piercing her ear. "Word on the street is that you're here because you've got a problem with your boss."

God, he hated small towns.

"And you shouldn't give too much weight to rumors," he added. "Small towns might thrive on them, but they're rarely rooted in fact."

"So you weren't sent here as punishment?" she asked, her tone as friendly as her face was curious. Whether it was a ploy to garner gossip fuel, or whether she was actually interested, Diego couldn't tell.

He'd been about to write her off as a sexy nice girl. Sweet, but not much of a challenge. Now he wasn't so sure of anything but the sexy part. That bothered him. His gift for reading people was one of the keys behind his success.

"I was sent here for two reasons," he said slowly, measuring just how much to share with the town pipeline. He might be having trouble getting a gauge on the pixie, but he knew how to finesse information. "I'm up for a major promotion. Solving this case is the last step to ensure I get it."

Diego had no problem lying to solve a case, but it was always easier to go with the truth if possible.

"And the second reason?"

It only took two steps for Diego to cross the room, standing close enough that the scent of her, light and airy, wrapped around him. For a second he forgot what he was doing. Forgot why he was there. Forgot everything except the sudden discovery of just how appealing sweetness could be.

Her lashes fluttered, thick and dark, hiding those expressive eyes. He watched the pulse quiver in her throat, wanting nothing more than to lean closer and press his lips to the soft flesh. To feel her heart race beneath his tongue.

As if reading his mind, she gulped. Then, as if she was trying to make it look casual, she moved over to the armoire, putting breathing distance between them.

Dammit.

"You were telling me the second reason you were sent here," she reminded him breathlessly.

To find out how many different sounds she could make while he brought her to orgasm? Diego gave himself a mental head slap and tried to shake off the sexual fog.

"The second reason? Because I'm good," he promised.

Her eyes widened, fingers clenching the wicker handles of the laundry basket so hard it made a loud snap. Grinning, Diego nodded. "I'm damn good. I close cases, and I put criminals away. Whoever did this, their ass is mine."

And there ya go. Toss in a little intimidation, and he'd be home by the end of the weekend. Before he did anything stupid, like give in to the need to find out if the pretty little blonde's naughty side was reserved for her lingerie.

"You promise?" she asked, looking around the mess of her bedroom. "You'll find out who did this. And why?"

Diego didn't do promises. Growing up, he'd had too many broken to ever want to cause someone else that kind of disappointment.

He looked around the room. The deputies who'd been called in on the previous burglaries had dusted for prints and come up bust. Despite the shift in M.O. from snatch-and-run to destruction, there was no reason to think this time'd be any different. This was either a copycat with a grudge against Ms. Carson, a totally unconnected case, or all the other thefts had been smoke. Which meant the green-eyed pixie was the real target.

He'd have to work the case as if all three were fact. But his gut said it was the latter. He just had to find enough evidence to pull all the pieces together. And he would. Because that's what he did.

But the pretty little blonde was looking at him as if he had a superhero cape tucked under his leather bomber jacket. Diego was a good cop. A damn good one. But no one had ever considered him a hero.

It was weird. And very appealing.

And probably his downfall, since he couldn't resist leaning closer and reassuring her.

"Babe, I guarantee it."

5

THREE HOURS AFTER he'd made that promise to Jade, Diego tossed his gym bag onto a creaky bed in a cramped room and sighed. His stomach ached from cookie overload. His head hurt from holding back his investigative instincts and trying to follow Kinnison's damn rules.

He would bet his Harley that Kinnison didn't realize how badly he'd screwed over his recalcitrant detective. Dumping him in a town so small, they didn't even have a cheap motel. Instead, he was stuck holing up in some old guy's spare room. Because, apparently, as much as the ladies of the town might like the safety of having a man around their home for a few days, *it wasn't proper.*

So now, he eyed the twin bed with its threadbare Speed Racer comforter and stingy pillow. It looked as if he'd have a backache to round it all out.

And what did he have to show for it?

Five interviews with four victims and one interested party—namely, a grizzled old woman by the name of Mary Green. Two tins of cookies, one of fudge and a question-able fruitcake—again from Mrs. Green. And a lecture on the lost art of saying please and thank-you.

What he didn't have to show was any more information.

None of the women had been home during the thefts. None had recently been involved in any sort of conflict, either alone or with each other. They didn't wear the same brand underwear, do laundry at the same place or shop together.

Other than living in the same small town, and as Jade had pointed out, all wearing feminine underthings—which had been painful for all parties to learn during his interview with Ben Zimmerman—there was no common thread.

Not even the type of underwear stolen. Everything from white cotton to something named after spankings—which neither he nor the mayor had been willing to ask about. If the selection left behind at Jade's was anything to go by, the thief had added supersexy to the collection.

Jade.

Diego dropped to the bed, wincing as springs that were likely as old as he was creaked loudly. It all came back to her. Every victim he'd talked to, he'd thought of her. Of how devastated she'd been when she'd seen the destructive mess in her bedroom. The other burglaries had been obvious, all with an open dresser drawer, rumpled contents.

The other victims were older. Not elderly, but all over forty. Except Jade.

Finally, now that he was alone and out from under the constraints of rules and protocol, Diego let his instincts have free rein. Risking his eardrums to another squeak from the bedsprings, he lay back on the bed, folded his hands behind his head and closed his eyes.

In the course of his questioning, he'd asked each of the victims about their ties to one another, and to Jade. As he'd expected, they all knew one another. But he had been surprised at the effusive praise they'd all had for Jade—even Mrs. Green of the rock-hard fruitcake.

The familiar tingle sped down his spine as intuition, finally cut loose from regulations, flared to life.

That was it, he realized.

Respect.

Unlike Jade, the other victims had been shown respect. Not just in the lack of vandalism they'd faced. But in the clear purpose of their break-ins. Their underwear had been found on display, but more as a joke. In a rolled-up newspaper left on the diner counter, in someone's mailbox, hanging from the barber pole. He didn't think the display of Jade's panties would be quite as unassuming and nonthreatening.

He didn't know how—yet. But Jade Carson was definitely the center of this case.

Both because the boring, by-the-book investigation logically suggested it, and because his spine was tingling.

That wasn't all that was tingling. He still had the remnants of a horny hangover. Unlike most hangovers, two aspirin, hot coffee and a nap wouldn't do anything to relieve this particular tension.

Nope. This tension required one of two things.

Jade.

Or a more of a hands-on, do-it-yourself kind of remedy.

Not willing to give in to his body's screaming urge for one or the other, he got to his feet. Maybe he could pace off some of the pressure.

On his third trip around the sparse bedroom, his cell phone rang. Diego pulled it from his belt, glanced at the display and rolled his eyes.

The captain could tell it to voice mail.

Diego tossed the phone on the bed and kept on moving.

His pacing ended at the tiny, narrow window. He glared out at the view. With the black sky aglow with overexuberant Christmas lights, the tiny town was like something off a postcard. Or one of those irritating movies with their saccharine moral messages.

Then his gaze shifted. He stepped closer to the window, angling himself along one wall, and located Jade's cottage on the next street.

His body went into hyperalert mode.

The same way it did when he knocked on a door and was greeted with the barrel of a shotgun.

Two hard thumps of his head against the wall weren't enough to keep him from looking again.

At his direct view right into the lingerie sprite's bedroom.

It was too far away to see details. The room was a shadow. But Jade? She was vividly clear. Her skin glowing as if she was fresh from the shower, she wore a tiny pair of candy-cane-striped shorts and a tinier tank top.

His mouth watered when she bent down to touch her fingers to her bare toes, making the fabric of her sleep shorts stretch across the best ass he'd ever had the pleasure of peeping at.

She slowly rolled her spine upright. Arms stretched overhead, she twisted to one side. The candy-cane-striped material pulled tight over breasts gloriously full for a woman so tiny. She twisted to the other side, then she slid her foot up to her knee, straightened her leg, and caught ahold of her calf.

He almost whimpered when, her hands wrapped around her ankle, she raised her foot overhead

Damn, she was limber.

When she did the other side, his body hardened to a painful state. He needed to stop. He was a cop. Not a peeping pervert.

Before he could force himself away from the window, though, she bent over again. Then, in a sleek move, she flipped into a headstand. Her tiny tank top slid up her torso. Diego's mouth dried up like the Sahara. The top bunched up just above—below? Which was it with her upside down?—her breast.

He wasn't sure what to wish for. That the fabric finish its slide south. Or that it stop, safely there so he could keep his professional sanity.

Slowly, as if she knew he was watching and she wanted to torture him, she spread those gorgeous sleek legs of hers into the splits. Diego's dick was so hard, he was afraid he'd bust his zipper. The woman was doing upside-down splits.

Before he could cry, or explode, she dropped back to her feet. A quick finger tousle of that pixielike hair and she padded over to the bed. Then, because someone somewhere had the tiniest bit of mercy for his sanity, she snapped off the light.

Show over, the room pooled black.

Diego threw himself on the rickety bed with a groan. Who said Christmas wishes—especially the kind that earned a guy a truckload of coal—didn't come true.

PERCHED SO LONG on the wooden stool that her butt was numb, Jade leaned her elbows on the high library counter, scrolling through photos on the computer. Her focus in life might be fashion first, followed closely by empowerment in all its forms. But if five years in the library had taught her nothing else, they'd taught her the art of research. There was very little by way of information that Jade couldn't find.

Including, it seemed, photographs and information on a certain sexy detective. She sighed as she enlarged a newspaper shot of Diego Sandoval in track shorts, sneakers and little else. His bare chest was partially obscured by the T-shirt he was using to wipe his face, but the grainy black-

and-white photo did lovely justice to the rounded muscles of his biceps and shoulders.

Oh, baby. She waved her fingers in front of her face. She'd been right. He was built beautifully. Like a male underwear model.

He came across as a loner. All the information she'd found, which, admittedly, wasn't a lot, seemed to support the message of a guy who did life solo. But he participated in the Cops and Kids Olympics?

Winning, she noted after forcing her gaze off the photo and on to the text, in four different events. Her eyes actually teared up when she saw one event was swimming and they hadn't included a photo of him in swim trunks. Or—she licked her lips—maybe he'd worn a Speedo like the guys in the real Olympics. He had one, after all.

His name was mentioned in a few crime-beat articles, his commendations touted in the county newsletter, and that was about it. No Facebook page. No Twitter account. Nothing else coming up on Google. So unless she tiptoed across the line and checked one of those pay-to-stalk sites, that's all she was getting to aid her in figuring him out.

That, and her own impression.

Which was admittedly clouded by lust.

Still, she got the feeling that Diego Sandoval was exactly what he said. A good cop, who was definitely sexy as hell. And his sexiness had nothing to do with vanity, she figured. No, he seemed to regard his sexy body as a tool.

A tool she'd love to use a few times.

Without taking her eyes from the photo, she reached for her tea. She grimaced as the rich honey-laced caffeine slid down her throat. Lukewarm was so…tasteless. Boring, even. Honey was best heated up. Maybe drizzled over a set of rock-hard abs. She'd bet it tasted extra sweet licked off that body. Was he one of those "service me and be grateful" kind of guys? She didn't think so. She'd got the "best sex of your life" vibe from him. Which meant he'd be the kind who'd reciprocate with the honey licking.

Oh, to be licked by a man who knew what to do with his tongue. Who could use it gently, in soft swirling entice-ment. Or roughly, with voracious hunger. Or, oh, please, yes, with plunging strength, in a scream-inducing rhythm.

"Sweetie, are you sure you should be in this morning? You could have taken the day off, you know."

Crap.

Her face flushed and breath a little shaky, Jade ripped her gaze from the computer screen and her mind from its fantasy over Diego Sandoval licking warm honey from her naked body.

"I'm fine, Mom. I don't like laundry enough to take an entire day off to do it," Jade said, trying to lighten the worry lines etched in her mother's forehead. Opal Carson had seen enough stress in the last five years. She didn't need to be worrying about creeps fondling her daughter's undies.

"Still, you don't look like you got much sleep." Opal frowned up at her daughter from her motorized scooter. "You could have taken a half day, slept in a little."

"I'd rather be here, keeping busy," Jade said with a cheerful smile, hoping to redirect the conversation. "Be-sides, if I stayed away today, I'd have to come in tomor-row. And tomorrow's crafts day."

She gave an exaggerated shudder, rubbing her hands over the billowing sleeves of her shirt as if trying to over-come the horror.

"You know how I feel about crafts day, Mother. Don't make me face glue sticks and glitter. And sequins. Oh, the sequins."

Opal's lips twitched and she shook her head. "It's beyond me how a girl as creative as you could hate crafts."

"I have no imagination," Jade said, shrugging as she slid from the stool. Time to quit drooling in the name of research and get to work.

"Darling, you have the best imagination of anyone I know."

"That's because you're the best mother of anyone I know," Jade said, coming around the counter and bending to plant a loud kiss on her mother's cheek. "And I'm not at all biased."

"Jade—"

Dammit. Tension spiked through Jade's system, swirling through her temples as if it wanted to take up residence and start pounding away. Before it could, and more important, before her mother could voice whatever motherly concern had her frowning at her middle child, a voice interrupted.

"Excuse me, ladies?"

Jade turned, automatically stepping aside so her mom could maneuver the scooter around the desk to face the speaker.

Well, well. Look who was turning into her very own knight in leather armor. Detective Sandoval stood just inside the entrance, the morning sunlight filtering in behind him doing nothing to soften his bad-boy edginess.

She offered a wide, welcoming smile. It was only her mother's presence that kept her gaze from dropping to the front of his jeans to see if they fit as well as she remembered. Checking out a guy's package was definitely a nonparental event.

"Good morning, Detective Sandoval. This is my mother, Opal Carson." Just a little breathless, she introduced them with a wave in what she figured was her mom's general direction. Her mom might have been perched on the roof for all she could tell, though, she was so fixated on the sexy detective. "Mom, this is Diego Sandoval. He's the detective that Mayor Applebaum brought in to deal with the underwear thefts."

"Detective, it's nice to meet you."

"Ma'am," Diego greeted, shaking her hand with a quick smile that flashed enough warmth and charm to make Jade wish she was the panting type.

"I hope you're taking this case more seriously than the rest of the town."

"I take every case seriously. This one is no different." He had that perfect "just the facts, ma'am" tone. "I won't stop until I've found the creep who broke into your daughter's house."

His words were intent enough for Jade to settle against the counter, pretty sure her mother wouldn't send her to the Religious Studies section to get a bible for him to swear on.

"And you're good at your job?" Opal asked, making her daughter groan.

"The mayor has access to my service history. He's spoken with my captain, who I'm sure gave a full and honest reference." He paused, an indecipherable look flashing across his face. Then he tilted his head toward the phone on the counter. "I have no problem with you taking your questions to the mayor. Actually, I'd appreciate it. The quicker people cooperate, the quicker I'll solve this case."

"I'll be talking with Mayor Applebaum this afternoon."

Even though he'd told her to do just that, Jade cringed at her mother's words. Diego smiled, though, and gave a satisfied nod. Then his gaze flicked toward Jade. "I'll be happy to answer any questions you have after your discussion. In the meantime, I need a few minutes with your daughter. I have some follow-up questions pertaining to last night's burglary."

"Take her home," Opal directed, waving her hand toward the door. "I've been trying to talk her into going, but she doesn't listen to me. You're an officer of the law, so you can force her to listen to you."

"Mom!" Jade exclaimed.

"It would actually be a lot more convenient if I could take another look at the crime scene."

Take him back to her bedroom?

Images of the two of them, naked and covered in honey, slid through her mind. She tucked them into the corner, knowing she couldn't enjoy them or their yummy effect while in the same room as her mother.

"I'll be back after lunch," Jade muttered, grabbing her purse from the cubby beneath the counter and slinging the long leopard-print strap across her chest. Diego followed her up the steps. She reached for the door, but before she could pull it open, his large hand covered hers. Warm, callused, intense, his touch sent shivers of desire spiraling through her body. Her legs tensed, heat pooling between her thighs.

Oh, please, let it be a honey-drenched lunch, she wished as the cool morning enveloped them.

Diego gratefully slid his sunglasses onto the bridge of his nose. Not in defense against the winter sun's weak rays. But because he needed something between him and the pretty little pixie. Her mouth was as clever as her looks were sweet.

He hadn't been able to get her—or those stretching moves she'd unknowingly tortured him with the previous night—out of his mind. A first for a noncriminal.

"So how does a detective go about solving a case like this?" she asked, pulling him from his thoughts. "Visit each house in town and inspect their underwear drawers?"

Although he'd ridden his Harley to the library, he didn't mention it as they walked past, toward the sidewalk. Walking was better. More exercise, a safe distance between their bodies. And, he noted as a set of curtains twitched when they passed a quaint A-frame, lots of witnesses. On the Harley, she'd have her arms wrapped around his body, her chest pressed to his back, and he'd likely drive right out of town to the nearest motel where he could beg her to switch positions.

Behind the pseudo safety of his dark glasses, he let his eyes eat her up. Her hair was just as tousled today as it'd been the day before, spiked ends thick around her shoulders and the bangs a sweeping tousle across one eye. Green earrings, a perfect match for her eyes, dangled to her jaw. Under the weathered leather jacket, she wore a black cotton shirt, the collar flipped up to frame her throat. Red lace peeked through the unbuttoned front of the shirt.

The black shirt was huge, hanging halfway down her denim-clad thighs. She'd wrapped a skinny red belt twice around her waist, so despite its size, the fabric followed her curves instead of hiding them. But it was the boots that held his attention. The woman had a way with boots. Black, again, these were flat-heeled and the suede over-the-knee style.

Sexy bohemian, was all he could think.

Very, very sexy bohemian.

His gaze met hers again.

"What're you doing here?" he wondered aloud.

Both her brows arched as she gave him, then the holiday-festooned neighborhood, a questioning look.

"I mean, you don't seem like a small-town type of woman."

Her eyes dimmed. Lashes fluttering, she slid her gaze toward the ground as if she was afraid the sidewalk was going to buckle at any moment. After a second or two, she gave a one-shouldered shrug.

"This is my home. I was born here, grew up here. My family is here."

Wondering why any of that would tempt someone to stay in a place that clearly didn't suit them, he looked around. Old houses, old people, no nightlife, more twitching curtains. Nothing worth sticking around that he could see.

"So that's it?" he clarified. "Roots and family ties?"

He almost wanted to hand her his sunglasses so she could hide the stricken look that swam in her bright gaze. Not so much for her sake, but for his. Seeing it made him want to slay dragons, kick asses and offer hugs. Clearly he was going crazy.

Then she puffed out a breath as if she was blowing away the urge to run, and shrugged. "It is what it is. The why doesn't matter."

A sentiment he usually lived by.

So why did it bother him so much to hear it from her?

Then she gave him a big smile.

"But hey, the upside is I know everyone in town. And I know everything about everyone in town," she said, her words rising with excitement. "You know what that means, right?"

"That privacy is a myth in Diablo Glen?"

Her laugh was like a bell, bright and cheery.

"Well, yeah, but that's a good thing because it means I can really help you out," she offered, placing an enthusiastic hand on his arm. "I'll introduce you around, lay the groundwork so people will talk to you, let you know if you're getting the facts or works of fiction. It'll be great."

Great?

He glanced at her hand, so small and slender on his arm. He couldn't feel her warmth through the leather of his sleeve, but he swore tiny sparks of electric heat shot from her fingers through his body, setting fire to all his erogenous zones.

Was she trying to kill him? First she made him think he was a superhero, making the first promise of his life. Then the almost-naked stretch session the night before that'd given him more aches than the too-uncomfortable-to-be-believed Speed Racer bed. Now this? As much time with her as he wanted, all in the name of solving a case?

"Thanks, but I work alone."

"Well, sure. But this is a special circumstance, right? I have something you need, and I'm happy to share it." Her smile teetered somewhere between sexual temptation and friendly encouragement.

"I appreciate the offer, but I'll be fine without help."

With a look somewhere between exasperated and amused, Jade shrugged. "Okay. But if you want easier entry, a smoother experience and quicker satisfaction, you just give me a yell."

His body hardened as heat flashed, forbidden and sweet.

Yep. She was trying to kill him.

6

DIEGO HAD NEVER ACTIVELY, desperately craved a woman the way he craved Jade at that moment. Had never needed to bury his face in the tender curve of her throat and breathe in her essence to see if it was as sweet as he thought. Resisting her when they were alone in her house would put all his cop training to the test.

"Holy crap," she breathed, stopping so fast he was surprised she didn't slam face-first into the sidewalk. Had he thought that out loud? He watched her eyes round in slow, horrified increments.

"What?"

Jade sprinted down the sidewalk so fast, Diego didn't know if she even heard him. As he stepped forward, the huge tree no longer blocked his view of her front yard.

He winced. "Holy crap, indeed."

Her house looked as if it was waving its sexy flag. The front lawn, porch and a few bushes were all sporting lingerie. Panties here, bras there. A single black stocking dangled from a wind chime.

Another hit? Diego didn't change his pace. No point since the apparent culprits were still in the front yard, both gathering lacies before the chilly wind could grab them away.

Jade didn't seem too worried about her lingerie blowing in the wind, though. She stormed right past the pretty little blonde trying to pluck a bra down from a naked tree branch.

"What the hell are you doing?" she snapped at the guy on her porch, one tennis-shoe-clad foot propping the screen open while he quickly tossed handfuls of undies inside. The guy straightened so fast his shaggy brown hair hit him in the eyes.

"We're sorry," the blonde said before Shaggy could defend himself. "I felt horrible when I heard what happened to your lingerie. I knew you'd be totally ooked out, so I came over this morning to take it to Mom's to wash. I was bringing it back and had my hands full."

Mom's? Reaching the front yard, Diego studied the other woman. Twenty at the most, she was as blonde and tiny as Jade, but softer. Girlie curls tumbled around a face rounder, but no less striking, than her sister's. A pale blue skirt floated around her feet, matching the cloud-soft-looking sweater peeking out from her long, white wool coat. There was a third Carson sister, wasn't there? Diego scratched his chin, wondering if the gene fairy had been just as generous with that one, too.

"I tripped going up the steps, though," the pretty blonde said, almost in tears as she rose to her feet and angled one leg to show the dirty rip at the hem of her skirt. "The basket flew out of my hands and your unmentionables went everywhere. Oh, Jade, I'm so sorry."

"I'm not worried about the underwear, Beryl. I want to know where my cat is," Jade snapped, not looking pacified at all. Diego was impressed. He considered himself hardened and tough, but he'd have had trouble resisting the pleading sweetness in the younger woman's look. Must be some kind of sibling immunity.

"I thought I was helping," Shaggy excused sullenly from the porch. Ignoring Diego, he crossed his arms over his expensive ski jacket and gave Jade a look just as pouty as his girlfriend's. Diego couldn't help grinning. The pair of them looked like the last two sad puppies in a pet-store window on Christmas Eve.

"Helping? I'm under strict orders by the mayor, and by Mom, to keep Persephone inside for a reason," Jade scolded as she swept her hand toward the house next door. Diego followed the gesture, then winced. The cute wooden gingerbread house was lying on its side, tinsel shredded around a mangled foam candy cane.

"Neal didn't mean to let her out," the other woman explained quietly as she drew herself up. She gave Diego a curious look, but kept her focus on pacifying her sister. Tilting her chin so the curls slid over her shoulder, she waved her hand in a move worthy of any prom princess. "Neal was carrying some gift boxes that I wanted to hide here so Mom couldn't find them. Suddenly Persephone got all crazy. Growling at him and hissing and stuff. Then I tripped and when he came out to help me, she just sort of took off. You know how she is this time of year."

Was the cat really that bad? He cast a quick, suspicious glance around the bushes, glad to be wearing thick leather motorcycle boots. Just in case.

"She's supposed to stay inside," Jade said stiffly, as if she was having to filter her words through her teeth to keep the cussing at the back of her tongue.

Diego knew the feeling.

"We'll catch her," the princess offered. "I promise, we'll haul her back before she does any damage."

"She headed for the park. She'll probably go straight for

the gazebo. I'll get her before she can haul any decorations off. Don't worry, I'll fix it," Neal said, his words conciliatory, despite the flash of anger in his eyes. He brushed a quick kiss on the princess's cheek, then sprinted down the steps and across the street without glancing left or right. Arrogance? Or that small-town lack of basic caution necessary to survive in the city?

"I'm so sorry," Jade's sister said again. "I wanted to have this done before you got home. I knew you were upset after the break-in. I didn't mean to make it worse."

"I know, sweetie," Jade said with a sigh, shoving her hand through her hair so the ends danced every which way. "I appreciate you trying to help. Especially since laundry's your least favorite chore. But you know how unreasonable everyone gets about Persephone this time of year. I'm going to be hearing complaints for days now."

"People overreact," the princess dismissed. "Just because she rearranges a few displays, they get all bent out of shape."

Diego arched a brow at the mangled tinsel and broken gingerbread display. Rearranges?

"She's only bad in December," Jade excused with a worried look at the park. Then she glanced at Diego and winced. "I'm so sorry. Detective, this is my sister Beryl. Berry, this is Detective Sandoval. He's the panty cop."

"Nice," Diego said with a grin. He glanced at the black silk panties caught on a bush and quit smiling. His body tightened as he considered how many ways he'd like to conduct an in-depth investigation of Jade's underwear.

Oblivious, the younger woman gave Diego a quick smile, then cast a nervous look toward the park where her boyfriend had disappeared. She bit her lip, before giving her sister a beseeching look. "I'm sorry, but I've got to go help him. I'm afraid Persephone might be hard to catch. She doesn't like Neal very much for some reason."

With that and another quick hug for Jade, she rushed toward the park. As if her sister's departure had let the air out of her, Jade seemed to deflate. Her smile dropped, her shoulders sank and her sigh was pure stress.

"Your cat isn't the friendly sort?" he asked, not because he cared but because he hated seeing that look of distress in her eyes again.

"Actually she is, usually. There's something about this time of year, though," Jade explained. "She was a feral I rescued when she was three months old. In January it'll be four years. I don't know what she went through over Christmas, but it seems to have made a lasting impression and she's been trying to dish out paybacks ever since."

Diego laughed.

"You wanted to ask me some questions, though, not to hear about my crazy cat," she remembered with a wince. "Let's go inside and I'll make you some hot cocoa and you can do whatever you need to do. I'll deal with this when we're finished."

Diego shook his head. "You go ahead and deal with this. It's probably better that you clean it up as quick as you can. I'll catch up with you later."

She glanced at the stocking waving in the chilly air and grimaced. "You're probably right. But I want to help you, too."

"I'll catch up with you later," Diego repeated, leaving before he could change his mind.

Later, when and where there were plenty of other people around. Diego didn't believe in fate or luck, but he wasn't going to spit in the face of a chance to sidestep disaster.

And the pretty blonde with the sexy underwear?

She had disaster written all over her. At least, disaster for his peace of mind, possibly his career, and definitely the fit of his jeans.

FOUR HOURS LATER, Diego's head pounded with tension. He poked at his temple with a stiff finger. His hands ached. In part from the cold weather—apparently a visiting cop in a small town was a suspicious character who had to stand on the porch for interviews. In part from spending the last four hours clenching his fists to keep from lashing out.

Standing outside the café, he debated getting a cup of coffee, then figured he needed to walk off the frustration instead of fueling it with caffeine.

He'd been stonewalled. No two ways about it.

And it was frustrating the hell out of him. You'd think he'd be used to it. He figured people slamming doors in his face, shooting at him and, on one memorable occasion, trying to run him over were all part of the job description. But this was different. These weren't criminals, they were nice, run-of-the-mill citizens. Who wouldn't talk to him.

Diego shoved his fists in the pockets of his jacket as two more of those nice, run-of-the-mill citizens crossed to the other side of the street when he passed. Like, what? He had out-of-towner cooties? Or maybe they thought he'd shoot them. Typical small-town close-mindedness, he sneered. The same kind he'd seen over and over as a kid.

And just like when he'd been a kid, he was stuck here until some official deemed him good enough to move on.

Diego gritted his teeth so hard, he hoped this Podunk town had a dentist. He was gonna need one before the end of the week.

How the hell was he supposed to get information if he had to wear kid gloves? He wasn't a kid-glove kind of cop, dammit. He felt both blindfolded and hamstrung. There was no way he was going to make progress playing nice.

He kicked a rock out of his path. A woman on the opposite sidewalk gathered her kid close, as if he'd kick it next.

He was seriously starting to hate this town.

Except for the sexy pixie. For her, he had some solid nonhate feelings brewing. But like his tried-and-true methods of solving a case, she was off-limits. Because she didn't just play nice, she was nice.

He wondered how deep that layer of nice went. Was it a surface thing? Or was she nice through and through? He had a feeling—mostly brought on by his body's intense reaction to her—that there was something naughty going on beneath the surface.

The question was…how naughty?

"Naked before the third date" naughty?

Or "whipped-cream bikini" naughty?

He thought about the pair of tiny black silk panties he'd fondled twice now. His body stirred, hardening in salute to the memory. A woman who wore black silk with tiny red roses? She might be convinced to try on some whipped cream.

Grinning at the prospect, Diego was a heartbeat away from convincing himself that pursuing the sexy pixie wouldn't have any effect on his ability to solve this case. Or more important, to solve it by Kinnison's stupid rules.

"Detective."

Glancing over his shoulder at the greeting, Diego slowed his pace to a halt. Then, with a barely discernible sigh, he came to attention.

"Sir," Diego greeted when the older man reached his side. "I'd planned to find you this afternoon to discuss the case."

"Great minds, and all that," Mayor Applebaum said,

gesturing for Diego to continue his walk. The older man took control of the direction, though, heading for the park. And, Diego noted as they passed a few more wary citizens, some semblance of privacy.

"So, how is your investigation going?" the mayor asked as they reached the grassy area.

Diego debated. Then, with his usual tact, he stated, "It's sucking. Sir."

Applebaum's lips twitched as he gave a slow, contemplative nod. He looked around as if the bench choices were of prime importance before settling himself on the one in the sunshine.

And waited.

Diego sighed. Realizing he had no choice, he dropped to the bench, too.

"I've had a few phone calls this morning, Detective."

Shit. He'd been on his best behavior. He hadn't intimidated a single person. So why were they whining?

"Sir?"

"People are a little put out that I'd bring an investigator in for what most see as a joke."

"Yep." Diego nodded. "I can understand their position." Applebaum didn't bother to hold back the grin this time.

"Still, it's my decision to make. I want this solved. The prank element doesn't bother me. But there is a meanness involved here, son. Oh, sure, a lot of folks think it's innocent enough. But for the ones with their unmentionables hanging in the diner window…? They aren't so dismissive."

Diego thought about Jade's face when she'd seen the mess made of her bedroom. Prank or not, the mayor was right. Mean—and malicious.

"The problem is," the mayor continued, pulling out a pipe and tapping it against his knee but not lighting it, "you're an outsider. Whether embarrassed or dismissive, it's hard for people to talk to an outsider."

"You knew you'd be bringing in an outsider when you called Kinnison."

"Yep. I did."

The older man looked toward the center of the park, with its big white gazebo and prettily decorated Christmas tree. Then he gave Diego a big, friendly smile.

Diego felt as if he was looking down the barrel of a gun, not sure if it was loaded or not.

"So here's what I'm thinking. You want to get this case solved, go on home before the holidays and get on with your life."

All right, except for the holidays part.

"With the break-in and destruction at Jade's, the situation is escalating. So the sooner this case is solved, the better for my town."

And...?

"To accomplish that, I've come to the conclusion that you need a little help."

A little help. Diego shook his head. Apparently the good mayor didn't believe in pointing a weapon unless it was loaded.

"Not someone telling you how to do your job," Applebaum assured him. "Not someone like me who everyone will be on their best behavior with. That's not likely to help you much."

Diego narrowed his eyes. The old guy was smarter than he looked.

"What you need is an intermediary. Someone the townspeople like and respect. Someone who can put them at their ease, as well as give you insight into whether or not they're being truthful."

"I don't need people at ease," Diego said between clenched

teeth. "Nor do I need someone to tell me something I've been trained to observe myself."

"'Course you don't." The mayor tapped the pipe against his knee again before bringing it to his mouth and making a show of lighting it. A couple puffs, and he gave Diego a stern look through the sweetly scented smoke. "But it'd make me feel a whole lot better."

Trapped and screwed over, all at the same time. Diego wondered if this was how prisoners felt when the doors of the cell slammed closed.

RESTLESS, JADE SLAMMED one book after the other into a stack, taking great satisfaction at the noise. She'd played on her favorite website for a while, putting outfit after virtual outfit together. Until she'd realized all the outfits were designed for seducing a very uninterested detective. Then playing stylist had lost its appeal.

What good was Santa if he sent her the perfect man for perfect sex, but that man wasn't into her? It was like wrapping a remote-control race car in bright, fancy paper and putting the biggest, brightest bow on top. And not including the remote.

Typical to her life, she supposed. She glanced around and sighed. Just like this job. The library was nice enough. One of the prettiest buildings in Diablo Glen. Solid oak graced not only the floors, but the gleaming rows of tall bookcases and a dozen cozy tables. The chairs were the kind a person could sink into for hours, and the art on the walls were originals. Shooting off four of the walls in the octagonal room were arched halls, each labeled with a hand-carved wooden sign.

It was rich and warm and welcoming.

And felt like a prison.

"My Humps" rang out, pulling Jade from her funk.

At least the prison came with phone privileges. She snickered as she answered her cell.

Ten minutes later, she tossed the phone back in her purse and stared at the pages of notes she'd made.

"Good news, dear?"

"I'm not sure." Frowning, Jade shrugged before glancing toward her mom. "It was the administrative office at the community college. They invited me to do a series of guest lectures next semester."

Opal clapped her hands together, beaming with pride as she wheeled toward her daughter. "Darling, that's wonderful."

"It'd only be six classes, not a full load," Jade said, trying to decide if she was excited or not. "I'd have to send a course description and syllabus for approval."

Was this a good thing? A part of her was doing handstands. But another part was settling in for a deep pout, since this was yet more evidence that she wasn't living in a big city, working as a stylist to the rich and famous.

"A description and syllabus shouldn't be difficult. Would you use the empowerment workshops you've already taught here, or come up with something new?"

"I'm not sure yet," Jade said, staring at, but not seeing, the counter.

She loved the workshops here, and it'd be fun to take the message wider. Empowerment Through Fashion. Know Yourself, Know Your Style. Tried-and-True: Wardrobe Staples and Attitude Standards. It was a good opportunity. A chance to really expand her workshops and reach a lot more people.

Possibly a whole new career direction.

But she already had enough issues feeling like a fraud here in her small hometown. Would a bunch of people want to pay good money—at a college, no less—to listen to a woman who wanted to be a fashion stylist, but wasn't empowered enough to go for the dream?

"I'll have to think about it," she finally said, her throat so tight it was hard to get out the words. "It's no biggie either way."

Opal gave her a look that said she clearly saw the flashing chicken sign over her daughter's head. But she let it pass. She'd been letting a lot of things pass lately, Jade realized. She frowned at her mother, noticing that she was not only wearing a new shade of lipstick, but one of her best day dresses that Opal usually saved for church. Before Jade could ask what was up, though, her mother gave her watch a pointed look.

"My shift is finished and I'm meeting…um, someone for lunch," Opal said quickly, an attractive wash of pink coloring her cheeks and making Jade frown. What was her mother up to?

"Marion is due in an hour to relieve you. You go home when she gets here, Jade. Don't let her guilt you into thinking that taking a couple of hours off this morning is something you have to make up for by staying late."

If it was anyone but Marion, Jade might have.

Before she could make a snarky remark, or her mother could offer up any more warnings, the doors opened.

"Home in an hour," Opal said quietly as she turned her scooter toward the door to leave. The quiet whir of the motor stopped short when she saw who'd come in. A quick glance back at her daughter showed she was struggling, but after a deep breath, she continued toward the exit.

"Thank you," she murmured to the man holding the heavy oak door wide.

Jade waited until the doors shut behind her mother before letting the excitement building in her tummy spiral through the rest of her body.

"Good afternoon, Detective Sandoval. What a pleasure. What brings you back my way so soon?" Her question was innocent. The low, husky, flirtatious tone was anything but. She leaned her forearms on the high counter, tilting her head to one side, liking the way the bright afternoon light streamed through the library windows, the watercolor effect of the stained glass surrounding him in an ethereal glow.

Maybe Santa hadn't done her wrong?

Then again, the good detective was standing at the steps by the door, not budging an inch closer. A gift she had to work for? Hmm, she considered. Well, for one that fine, she was willing to expend a little effort.

"I just spoke with the mayor," Diego said, not looking as if it'd been a fun conversation. Jade was surprised. Applebaum had a way about him that people usually enjoyed.

"Do tell?" she invited, figuring he wouldn't have mentioned it if there wasn't something in the conversation that pertained to her. The detective just wasn't the sharing type.

"He seems to think that the investigation would go smoother, faster, if I had an intermediary."

Eyes rounding, Jade shot her brows up. She pressed her lips together to keep from grinning. Her toes wiggled in her boots, but she managed to still them as well. Nope, no happy dancing. It might change his clearly teetering mind.

"Does he?" she said as soon as she was sure she wouldn't sound as though she was gloating. "What sort of intermediary?"

The look he shot her said he knew exactly what her toes were doing and he wasn't happy about it. Still, he moved the rest of the way into the room, stopping just a foot from the counter. Must be in appreciation for her attempted restraint.

"Oh, you know. Someone to introduce me around, lay

the groundwork so people will talk to me," he said stiffly, throwing her words back at her. "Someone who can gauge whether people are telling me facts or fiction."

A giggle escaped before Jade could stop it. Her hand flew to her mouth, but it was too late. His frown turned into a scowl. But she saw the light in his dark eyes. Oh, yeah, that was amusement in those sexy depths. She was sure of it.

"I swear," she said, holding up one hand as if taking an oath, "I didn't call him. After seeing my lingerie take the outdoor tour, I forgot about it."

Which was pretty much the truth. Well, she'd mentioned it in passing to her mom, but only as a setup to the "coming home to see her panties dangling from the eaves" story.

"Fine. I'll take your help. But first we need to get a few things clear."

Before he could get to those things, though, a wince-inducing squeak filled the room.

They both turned to watch Mrs. Green push a book cart, the top shelf covered in brightly colored romance novels, most with half-dressed couples looking as if they were going to jump each other. Jade made a mental note of a couple of the positions, hoping she'd get a chance to try them out soon.

"I've got my books for the week, Jade. Can you check me out? Carrie will be here any minute now to pick me up." She squeaked the cart to the edge of the tall counter. Then, a little breathless, she peered up at Diego through her tiny round lenses. "Detective. Are you here looking for clues?"

"Just checking with Miss Carson for some background information on a few things." He hesitated a second, then, with the same look the neighbor boys had worn when caught smashing pumpkins two months before, he helped the elderly woman shift her book selection from the cart to the counter.

Jade's heart turned to goo.

"Ah, good idea. Our Jade is a fount of information."

Mrs. Green reached across the counter to pat Jade's hand, then snapped her fingers. "Or, if that doesn't work, the mystery section is quite extensive. I suggest you look to Miss Marple for ideas."

Diego's hand froze, his expression baffled. Jade ran her tongue over her front teeth, hoping the threat of biting it would keep the grin at bay.

Who? he mouthed.

Jade tilted her head. Following her direction, Diego glanced to the left. A portrait of a woman in a large, ornate gold frame hung on the wall. The plaque beneath it said Agatha Christie.

His gaze shot back to Jade. She busied herself checking out the books to keep her hand from patting his cheek. He was such a big, bad, tough loner, but there was something about Diego that made her want to cuddle him close.

"Um, thanks," he said. "I'll keep that in mind."

There it was. That was why she wanted to cuddle him. Because for a big, bad, tough loner, he was just about the sweetest, most sensitive man she'd ever met.

"See that you do." Mrs. Green gave a sharp nod in emphasis, then took the bag Jade held out, huffing a little at the weight. "Thank you, dear."

Diego nodded goodbye. The look he gave Jade warned that she keep all comments to herself. Since most of the ones floating through her brain were sappy and sweet, she didn't figure she wanted to share anyway.

"About that help," he said, stepping aside for the elderly woman to pass. As she did, Jade watched Mrs. Green's eyes drop, then a wicked expression crossed her wrinkled face. She could have warned him. But what was the fun in that?

The little old lady stopped right behind him, hesitated for just a second to give Jade a questioning look. Then, with a shrug that said life's too short to hold back, she reached out one gnarled, age-freckled hand and patted Diego's ass.

His eyes widened in shock. His body stiffened as if he'd just been hit in the head with a big stick.

The frown he gave Jade was ferocious.

Then, looking horrified, he turned to watch the little old woman toddle her way across the polished wood floor, her bag of sexy books over her arm and a candy-cane-striped scarf trailing down her back.

"That did not just happen," he vowed.

"Oh, it happened, all right." Jade laughed so hard she snorted. At his arch look, she clamped her hand over her mouth and, eyes sparkling with glee, tried to pull herself together.

"Oh, man, the look on your face," she said, wiping her eyes.

"That old lady just patted my ass," he said, nonplussed.

"Well, it's a nice ass," Jade said agreeably. "Surely it's happened before."

"I live in a big city. I'm surrounded by hundreds of thousands of people every day. I crawl through the dregs, the desperate and the depraved. But I can't remember the last time someone patted my ass."

Biting her lip, Jade watched him closely. It was one thing for her to think he had a soft, cuddly center. But he was still pretty much an unknown. And he'd just been fondled by a woman three times his age. He wouldn't do anything crazy, would he? Like chase the old woman down and write her a citation for inappropriate handling of an officer of the law?

"Should I be flattered?"

Relief and something else, something she was too scared to put a name to, poured through her.

"You should be flattered, in the sense that you do have a mighty pattable tush," she told him, giving her brows a playfully suggestive wriggle.

"But?"

She snickered at his play on words. "But, she pats my tushie, too. So it's not personal. Well, it is, in that it's your butt she's touching. But she wasn't making a move so much as showing affection."

"Affection?"

"Sure. She's babysat almost everyone in Diablo Glen at one point or another. Diapered most of us. Mrs. Green pretty much sees everyone as a little kid."

"That's kinda weird."

"That," she assured him, "is typical of Diablo Glen."

"You're on the clock, Jade," a voice said, coming from the employee entrance. "You can talk to your boyfriend on your own time."

Jade sighed. She turned to face her future in-law. As usual, Beryl's fiancé's mom Marion looked as if she'd woken up on the wrong side of the bed. Her iron-gray hair showed recent signs of a kitchen-shear trim, highlighting the deep creases between her brows. That's what years in an empty bed did to a woman. Jade rubbed her own forehead, wondering how long it'd take for her own scowl lines to etch in that deep.

Marion had arrived in Diablo Glen ten years ago, a single mom whose husband had run off, leaving her to raise Neal alone. Since then, she'd bought a large chunk of the land on the west side of town, harangued her way into a position of power in the community and hooked her son up with the prettiest girl in Diablo Glen—although Jade might be a little biased there. Despite her ferocious demeanor, she wasn't all bad. She regularly donated lovely handmade ethnic crafts and clothing to the local sales and every Christmas brought a feast of tamales, enchiladas and homemade tortillas to the Christmas party. Jade figured she saved her softer side for the revolving door of relatives that often landed on her property at the edge of town.

"Marion Kroger, Detective Sandoval with the sheriff's department," Jade introduced in lieu of a greeting or correction. After all, she wouldn't mind him being her boyfriend. Or man toy. Whatever. "The detective is here regarding the Panty Thief crimes."

"Don't give that ugliness a clever name, Jade. It only glorifies the rude act."

"Right," she said with a slow nod. "Okay, then. The detective is here to ask a few questions in relation to the recent series of unfortunate events."

Before the other woman could call her out on the smart reply, Jade looked back at Diego. "Detective, this is Marion Kroger. She volunteers here at the library part-time, and she's the chairwoman of Diablo Glen's Friends of the Library group."

"Detective," Marion greeted stiffly after bending low to push her handbag to the very back corner under the desk. "Does the sheriff really think it necessary to assign an officer for just one crime? Especially one as frivolous as this seems to be?"

Frivolous? Jade thought of the mess in her bedroom. The torn books, the lingerie strewn everywhere. Of how hard it had been to sleep there, in the room that'd once been her haven. The creepy feeling of being invaded, of violation. That didn't even take into consideration the two thongs and red satin panties that were missing.

Those, she figured, would cost her a few months of teasing, a lecture from her mother and probably a few heavy-breathing phone calls after they were publicly displayed.

Unless Diego solved the case first. She wasn't sure which she wanted more. For him to catch the creep before her panties were draped over Joseph's head in the town-square manger. Or to keep him around long enough for her to have her way with him—a few dozen times.

"I'm sure when all is said and done, it'll be found that this whole thing is some holiday hoax," Marion continued dismissively, primly restacking the books Jade had already sorted on the counter.

"The burglaries are real," Diego stated. "And thanks to the recent vandalism and destruction of property, the case has been upgraded from petty theft to an aggravated misdemeanor."

"Destruction? Vandalism?" Hands so freckled with liver spots they looked tanned, paused. Kroger gave Diego a hard stare, then folded her fingers together. "I didn't realize the problem had escalated to that degree. If this keeps up, we'll need an entire fleet of policemen here to protect us. What are you doing about this, Detective?"

"That's what Ms. Carson and I were discussing. The mayor suggested she help me out."

"Then what are you still doing here?" Marion asked Jade, giving her a shooing motion with her fingers. She looked around, ducked her head beneath the counter, then straightened and pushed Jade's purse into her hands. "Go. Help the detective. Do whatever it takes to catch the nasty little thief."

Well, then. No guilt trip over a short workday, no bitching about the books that hadn't yet been sorted. Jade made a mental note to jot that down in her diary. It was a first, after all.

"Shall we?" she said to Diego, giving him a flirty look

through her lashes. She'd be happy to give him a few other things, too, once they were in private.

The same spark of interest that'd made her tummy flutter earlier flashed in his eyes again before it was quickly banked.

He was such a challenge, clearly interested but just as obviously determined to resist the attraction.

Wouldn't it be fun to see which one of them won?

7

WHICH WOULD BE LESS PAINFUL? Bellied up to a rock? Or wedged between a hard place? Diego had his orders, from two bosses, no less. And both sets of orders sparkled like crystal. Solve the case, follow the rules and enlist Jade's help. Hello, rock.

When the crotchety old woman added a hiss to her glare, as if questioning why he was still breathing her air, he forced his feet to follow Jade toward the back of the library and what he was sure was a waiting hard place.

Clearly ignoring his concern about spending more time with her, he settled his gaze on the sweet rear view. Her shirt was too big and baggy, despite the cinched belt around the waist, to give a good look at her butt. But there was something hypnotic about the sway of her slender hips, the way those boots reached so high up her legs. His fingers itched to trace a path between the black suede and the full curves of her butt, draped under that crisp cotton.

Fantasizing now about which pair of panties he'd discover if he did, Diego barely noticed they'd left the building until the bright December sun smacked him in the face.

Blinking, he glanced around. A redwood pergola arched over the slate patio. Dormant winter branches climbed the posts, empty flowerpots were dotted here and there between benches. At the far end, opposite the door, was a small play area and covered sandbox.

"So, His Honor, the mayor, would like me to help on this case. But what about you, Diego? What do you want from me?" she queried, her look as innocent as her tone was naughty. Echoing the naughty, she stepped closer.

Close enough that he could smell the sweet spice of her perfume. Could count the row of tiny red gemstones curving around her earlobe, getting smaller as they rose toward her temple. Close enough that all he'd have to do was breathe deep to feel her breasts against his chest.

A fit she might not mind checking out herself. She looked as if she wanted to lap him up in a saucer, her eyes as satisfied as her cat's. But there was something else in her gaze. Something hesitant, almost afraid. Like she wanted him, but was worried that he might want her, too.

Nothing said *I want you to take me now, but stay the hell away* like that kind of look. The latter lined up perfectly with the warning siren going off in his brain. But the finger triggering that siren wasn't his. It wasn't Kinnison's or even Applebaum's. It was his conscience. Rarely let out to play, it was screaming *Nice girl*. And guys like him should stay away from nice girls.

Diego wondered if this was how he was going to go. Not a nice, clean bullet through the head or something that'd look heroic written up in the newspaper. Nope, he was going to die of sexual frustration brought on by a conflict between his body's desperate cravings and those nagging voices in his head. The voices wouldn't be so bad if they were in line with his own finely tuned sense of right and wrong. Instead, he had tight-ass nagging boss voice and avuncular old mayor with a worrisome resemblance to a talking cricket in a top hat.

As always when he was conflicted, Diego fell back on intuition. And his intuition was telling him that Jade Carson was as sweet as she was gorgeous, would be as wild in bed as she was amusing out of it. And that she was trouble, through and through, for a guy who planned on cruising through life alone.

Chilled for some reason, he stepped back, putting some distance between him and Jade. Something flashed in her big green eyes. Hurt? It was gone so fast, he couldn't tell.

It shouldn't matter. He shouldn't care.

But all he could think about was finding a way to bring joy back to her eyes, to make her feel happy again. Hell, he had to bite his tongue to keep from asking her if she wanted to talk.

To talk?

If his dick wasn't hard enough to drill railroad spikes right now, he'd wonder if he was turning into a girl.

Clearly, Jade was a serious threat to his sanity.

Diego steeled himself with the reminder that he was a loner. A hard-ass who didn't do relationships that required more depth than a paper plate. Bad news to any woman who considered a future past rolling out of bed in the morning.

Good enough. All he had to do was ignore that flash of heat, that almost kiss, those unnamed emotions in her eyes. As long as he did, she would keep her distance. Good girls were predictable that way.

Satisfied, and yeah, maybe a little smug, he prepared to fill her in on how he wanted this town-liaison role to work out.

Before he could say anything, she closed that distance between them again. He froze.

"I made you uncomfortable, didn't I?" Her smile pure

mischief, she reached out to give his upper arm a sympathetic pat.

"Don't be ridiculous." Nerves he hadn't realized he had exploded. Unfrozen, he took three steps back. Then another one just for good measure.

"You are uncomfortable. Nervous even." Her smile widened, delight dancing in her eyes. "It's not like I licked you or anything."

What the hell? Was she reading his mind and delighting in trying to blow all his preconceived perceptions to pieces? Diego could only shake his head. "You are one hell of a confusing woman. Did you know that?"

"Me?" She batted her lashes.

"It's not a good thing," he groused.

"Oh, but it is. You're so by-the-book, I'll bet you categorize, organize and file every single thing and person away in your mind. I like the idea of not fitting into a tidy little slot somewhere."

Diego frowned. "I'm not uptight."

"I didn't say you were."

"That description sounded pretty damn uptight to me."

"Was it wrong, though?" she teased.

Not sure if it was frustration over the unquenched thirst she inspired, or if it was ego demanding he show her just how un-uptight he was, Diego lost it. He actually heard his control snap like an overstretched rubber band.

He reached out and grabbed her by both arms, easily lifting her off her feet to pull her close again. She gasped. But she didn't look scared. She looked intrigued.

That was good enough for him.

"How uptight is this?" he growled just before his mouth took hers.

Jade's body melted against him, so slight, so soft. Her

arms rested on his shoulders for balance, her fingers lax. Her lips, sweet and yielding, didn't move.

Okay. So maybe he'd read her wrong. Or maybe this was how good girls kissed. Since she was his first, he didn't know.

She tasted delicious. Like warm honey with just a hint of something dangerously addictive. Needing one more sip before he let go of the fantasy, he ran the tip of his tongue slowly over her lower lip. Then he gave a gentle suck.

As if he'd turned a magical key, she went wild. Her fingers spasmed, then dug tight into his shoulders before sliding behind his neck to tangle in his hair and grip his head.

Her mouth opened, welcoming and eager. Diego dived into the deliciously warm depths, wanting to eat her up in fast, greedy gulps. Her tongue met his in an erotic dance. His breath sped up, his pulse raced. And his body hardened like steel. He needed more. Wanted it all.

His hands were still gripping her arms, though. His fingers ached to touch her. To feel her soft curves, to slide down the length of those gorgeous legs. To explore every hot, sexy inch of her body.

But he'd have to put her down to do that. And he wasn't sure he could force his fingers to release her. He'd never wanted anything, anyone, the way he wanted Jade right now. It was as if he'd suddenly discovered the most important, powerful elixir of life. Kissing Jade made him feel as though he could actually have happiness. Real, lasting happiness.

A bell rang out, faint but insistent.

Diego surfaced fast. As if someone had grabbed him by the scruff of the neck and yanked him out of the pool of magical elixir. He shifted, softening the kiss and tuning in to their surroundings again. Or, as Jade's tongue enticed his back into her mouth, trying to.

Why had he thought he should slow it down? He couldn't remember as the taste of her filled his senses again.

The phone chimed again, accompanied by a buzzing this time. Loud, grating and way too insistent.

"Shit."

Furious for losing control, and for being interrupted before he could lose more of it, Diego set Jade down with a thud. Ignoring her shell-shocked look, he stomped a safe two yards away.

"That's my cell phone. I have to take the call."

"Huh?"

His ego swelled almost as big as his dick at the sex-fogged confusion in her eyes.

The phone buzzed again. He glanced at the display.

Kinnison.

It was like getting kicked in the ass in an ice bath. And, he realized, exactly what he needed. A reminder to keep his hands, mouth—and any other body parts—away from temptation.

WATCHING DIEGO TALK on the phone, Jade's body trembled with the aftershocks of desire. All she could think of was how much she wanted Diego, covered in hot fudge and whipped cream. She'd never felt this way before. Anticipation, excitement, heat, they all tangled together.

It was too fast, though.

Wasn't it?

Her mind pointed out that sex, even fling sex with a passing hottie who fit every single one of her fantasy requirements, always had repercussions. Responsible women made sure they could handle the repercussions before they dived off the deep end. They thought through the consequences.

And they made sure they were dressed appropriately.

And since all Jade's good lingerie was being washed—
again—she was stuck in granny panties and a torn cotton mustard-yellow bra. Pretty much the unsexiest undies
she owned.

There. Shaking her hands as if she could fling off the
sexual tension, she gave a decisive nod. That should keep
her from giving in to temptation.

Feeling like one of the teenage girls she often lectured,
Jade tried to at least look calm. Sure, her stomach was
dancing. Her pulse was racing. Maybe anticipation was
doing questionable things to the bagel she'd had for break-
fast. But she didn't have to look as if she was freaked out.
Faking It with Fashion 101… Look good and people believe you *are* good. Or in this case, look confident and he
wouldn't realize her toes were shaking.

While a part of her wondered when she'd become obsessed with sex, or at least sex with Diego, the rest of
her—the parts that weren't racing, dancing or threatening
to spew—tried to remember everything she knew about
being strong and empowered. About taking charge and
going after what she wanted.

Clueless that he was front and center in her obsessive
mental debate, Diego ended his call and tucked his phone
into his pocket. She watched him stride across the slate,
legs long and lean in dark denim. Here he came, temptation in a leather jacket.

She tilted her chin high, pulled her shoulders back and
pressed one hand against her stomach. Strong and steady,
she was ready to face down temptation. How's that for
empowered? she thought as she mentally patted herself
on the back.

"We should get to work."

She frowned. What happened to temptation?

"Work?" She peered at his face. Closed, distant and almost chilly. Her gaze slid to the phone he was tucking into his pocket. Had someone died?

"Work. I need to solve this case and get back to my own life," he said.

If he'd sounded angry, or impatient, she'd have been able to dish it right back. But he simply sounded...gone.

The way he'd be as soon as he solved this silly Panty Thief case. Gone, back to his own life. His exciting world. His career and his dreams.

And Jade would be here.

Same life.

Same town.

Same unfulfilled existence.

Pressing her lips tight together to keep the sudden tears at bay, Jade rubbed her hands over her arms, wishing she'd thought to grab her jacket.

"You okay?" he asked, closing the distance for a brief second to sound concerned.

"I'm fine," she said, shrugging as if it'd knock the tension off her shoulders. "Just chilly. I have an extra coat inside, though."

"C'mon, then." He gestured toward the library door. "Get it so we can go talk to people. You said you'd be able to ease the way so they'd open up to me, right? Fill me in, gauge fact from fiction?"

"Sure thing," she murmured absently, stepping into the dimly lit back room and making her way to the employee break room where she kept a spare jacket.

Suddenly—and she didn't care how illogical the idea was—she was sure Diego was more than just a hot, sexy temptation for incredible sex. He was inspiration, and for more than kinky positions. Empowerment meant grabbing ahold of what you wanted, taking risks and learning new things.

She didn't know what she might learn from him, what he might spark in her. She just knew he represented freedom. Excitement. She might have to settle for a life without her fantasy career as a stylist, but here was a chance to have a few of her other fantasies.

The sexual ones.

She just had to figure out how to convince him to strip naked and start making those fantasies come true.

THREE HOURS LATER, she was still figuring.

"I think that's it," Diego decided as he flipped through his little police notebook. "We've talked to all the victims and their families, as well as everyone who discovered the stolen goods. Was that the entire population of Diablo Glen?"

"Well, a large part of it," Jade agreed, keeping step with him as he strode down the sidewalk of Main Street. "There are about two dozen people out of town for the holidays. Visiting family, vacations, that kind of thing. And there are a few families who live out on the edge of the city limits, but we'd have to drive to see them."

Nonplussed, he shook his head. "I can't believe you can get from one end of town to the other without needing car keys."

"We can't have spoken with everyone. What about all the rest? The ones you waved to in stores, the diner. Gathered at that big building on the edge of the park. All prettied up to look like it's made of candy? Was that the town hall?"

Jade smiled at his description. The town hall, heck, all the public buildings, looked great. She'd actually had fun watching his reaction, seeing the disdain slowly melt from building to building as he came to appreciate all the artistry in the thematic decorations.

"You talked to all the major players in the panty drama, and most of the minor ones," she assured him. "There are a lot of people who aren't even bystanders, though. You caught us at our busy season. Rebecca Lee's getting married the first week of the new year, so she's got a bunch of relatives visiting. A lot of the families have company in for the holidays, too. Our quaint small-town-Christmas thing holds major appeal for some people."

As much as she craved the big city, she couldn't imagine doing the holidays any other way. Looking intrigued, Diego stopped to read a flyer in the bookstore window that announced the Twelve Days of Books event, complete with gingerbread and hot cocoa.

"You get a lot of strangers through?" he asked, nodding to a Washington license plate as he tucked his notebook back in his pocket.

"Sure, some. Like I said, there are a lot of visitors for a small town this time of year. You met Marion Kroger in the library?" She waited until he nodded before continuing, "She's got at least a dozen or more people out at her place. She must have a huge family, because they cycle through at least three or four times a year."

"Any of them come into town?"

Jade shrugged.

"Probably. Every once in a while we get a few people I can't place. But not too often. That's not a stranger's car, for instance. That's Mrs. Green's grandson's, Eddy. He's studying engineering at Washington University."

For the first time since he'd taken that phone call outside the library, Diego looked directly at her. Jade shivered a little. It wasn't that she'd forgotten how intense his gaze was. Not really. But a few hours in his company without feeling it had a way of making a girl think she could handle it.

Silly girl.

"I need to go over my notes," he said, still studying her face as if he was weighing something.

"Ah, well, I guess playtime's over then." Despite her cheery smile and light words, Jade's shoulders sank. Sure, he'd spent the last few hours holding her at arm's length, as if afraid one touch, one look, would be all the invitation she needed to straddle his body and demand he finish that kiss. But she'd still had fun.

It'd been exciting to help out, and fascinating to watch him work. The way he led the discussions, asking questions in such roundabout ways she didn't think most people had a clue how much information they'd given him. Even she, who'd lived here all her life, had found out a few new tidbits today.

She'd also had some seriously delicious fudge, a hot toddy, three cookies and had gotten a new recipe for double-butter pound cake.

Even more exciting, she'd been asked to help two women find the perfect outfits for their Christmas parties, been recruited to do a styling workshop on dressing right for New Year's Eve and had been advised that she talked about sex too much.

Diego had choked on his cookie at the last one, she remembered with a grin.

Maybe she hadn't gotten any closer to him, as she'd hoped. And perhaps the adventurous, self-sufficient vibe he radiated hadn't rubbed off on her, as she'd wished. But it'd been a fun experience, and hey, an afternoon with a hot, sexy guy was never a bad thing.

Focus on the positive, she always told herself. Even if it didn't include another taste of the most tempting mouth she'd ever felt against hers.

So, forcing her chin up and her smile wider, she tilted her head to one side and said, "This was fun. And even though it still seems like a pointless crime, I hope I was able to help." All that in a single breath. Not bad. She inhaled slowly, preparing to force the goodbye past her lips next. Before she could, he tilted his head toward the other end of the street.

"I need to make sure I've got all my facts straight. Let's go to the diner," he suggested. "I'll buy you a cup of coffee and you can make sure I didn't miss anything."

A date? He probably didn't see it that way. Still, Jade's tummy danced in anticipation. Then the clock in the tall spear of the town hall caught her eye.

"The diner's closed," she said.

"It's only four."

"Holiday hours," Jade said with a shrug, her mind racing with possibilities. Despite her nerves—she'd never asked a guy out before—she blurted out, "But I have coffee at my place. We can go back there. You wanted to see the crime scene again anyway, didn't you?"

There you go, a subtle invitation into her bedroom and one she could totally deny if he freaked.

And if he didn't? Well, she'd just have to strip naked before he saw her ugly underwear.

IT TOOK CAREFUL SKILL to walk that thin line between instincts, cravings and pure stupidity. Diego told himself his toes were still firmly balanced.

Of course, anytime he looked at Jade, took in her sexy bod and gorgeous smile, the balance teetered. So much for that myth about long poles adding stability.

Diego sighed, torn between tying things up and taking a break to get his brain straight.

After his useless round of interviews that morning, he'd figured this case was pure crap. After his much more insightful, informative and productive—thanks to Jade—

round of interviews this afternoon, he was still sure this case was pure crap.

At least, intellectually he was sure.

But his gut was saying something different. Instinct screamed loud enough to drown out his desperate need to get out of this Podunk town and back to the faceless, nameless anonymity of a big city.

And Jade was the key.

She'd sparked something when she'd mentioned all the strangers in town. Now he needed to get more information from her, but without tipping her off. Until he figured out what it was his gut was sensing, he'd be keeping his instinct's tingles all to himself.

And, he warned his itching fingers, his hands. No touching the sexy blonde. No feeling the curve of her ass to see if it was as tight and smooth as it looked. No weighing the feel of her full breast against his palm to see how it fit.

His body hummed at the image. He shifted, trying to shake off the sensual spell the afternoon with Jade had cast over him.

The sooner he solved this case, the sooner he could get the hell out of here. Back to real life, to his shiny new promotion and yet another new start. The idea fell like a ball of lead in his belly, a dull and lonely ache. Too many Christmas cookies, he told himself.

To solve the case, he needed to toe Kinnison's line, which meant following Applebaum's directive to use Jade's help. Since Diego's own gut agreed, he figured that was three against one.

"Sure," Diego finally agreed, realizing he'd been standing there like a moonstruck idiot long enough. "Coffee and another look at the crime scene sound good."

And wasn't he the big brave cop, heading off to Temptation Central. But hey, he was armed. He could handle a tiny little blonde with a smart mouth. Just as long as she kept her lingerie hidden away.

8

DIEGO SAT in Jade's kitchen, staring across the table at the soft, furry features of Jade's cat, wondering what was wrong with the people in this town. Once they'd loosened up and quit seeing him as an outsider whose face needed to meet their closed door, they'd all had similar warnings to offer.

Watch out. Caution. Dire consequences.

And all because of this sweet kitty?

"Why is everyone so freaked about your cat?" he asked, glancing over from the lush, long-haired feline perched on the opposite chair toward Jade. "It's like they've all got different opinions on the correct color of lights to string from a house, whether a tree should be green, white, aluminum or fake, and who makes the best cookies. But the fact that the panty thefts are a joke and your cat is pure evil seem to hit a total consensus."

"Well, you have to admit, it's hard to take the thefts too seriously," she said over the sound of water running into a coffeepot. "And are they technically thefts if the panties are always returned?"

"They're usually being left in weird places, on display and used to mock their owners."

"*Mock* is a pretty harsh word." She pulled the coffee-maker away from the wall to pour in the water.

"There was a pair of black lace panties big enough for three toddlers to play in with the words *Do Me* on the ass hanging from the blow-up reindeer in front of the post office this morning," he reminded her. How was that a joke? Did this town have no sense of privacy? No secrets at all? Not even who wore what style underwear in what size? He'd always thought sizes were like their real weight and age to women, closely guarded secrets.

"I'm not saying it wasn't a little disturbing to find out that Mrs. Kostelec has the same panties that I do. But the whole thing seems more like a joke than a crime to me," Jade admitted, taking a bag of coffee beans from the fridge and pulling a grinder out of a drawer. Diego was busy reveling in the addictively rich scent of the grinding coffee, so it took a few extra seconds for her words to sink in.

"You're kidding, right?" he asked, not sure if he was amused or horrified. His gaze dropped to Jade's ass, covered way too much in that big black shirt. Did her panties have an invitation written in glitter, too? His mouth watered. Maybe there was something to be said for following directions.

"Nope, I really was disturbed," she confessed. After flicking the on switch, she glanced back. She frowned at his impatient look, then gave an edgy sort of shrug. "Look, I know it's serious, even if most people aren't taking it that way. I saw the mess in my bedroom. It was all I could do last night not to run over to my mother's instead of sleeping in my own bed."

The look on her face, nerves and just a hint of the fear he'd seen the day before when she'd walked into her bedroom, made him feel even worse.

"I know it's serious. But if I think about it too much,

I'm scared," she told him quietly. "It's easier to trust that you're going to catch this guy, that you're really good at what you do and to believe I don't need to worry."

He grimaced at the anxious look in her eyes. Wanting to make her feel better, he promised, "While I'm on the job, nobody's going to hurt you. Or your underwear. I promise."

What was wrong with him? He didn't do promises. But the way her face lit up made him feel pretty damn good. She gave him a smile that made him feel like a superhero, then followed it up with a teasing wink.

"So the rumors are true, hmm? I heard you're quite the hotshot." As she spoke, she stretched on tiptoe to get two large red mugs off the shelf overhead. Diego shifted as if to help her, then seeing her fingers hook the ceramic handles, he settled back in the chair to continue enjoying the view.

"I thought the rumor was that I was a crappy cop who was sent here as punishment." The idea of people thinking he sucked at his job and the reality of being sent to Podunk, Nowhere, both grated on his ego in equal measure.

"One of the many joys of small towns. We wear the same underwear styles and the gossip changes with the direction of the wind," she said, giving him a teasing look over her shoulder as she poured the freshly brewed coffee into the mugs. "Word that the mayor has been bragging about your arrest record and police skills is spreading fast. He really likes you."

A cozy sort of feeling warmed Diego's chest. He'd never looked for cozy before and suddenly it was oddly appealing. The mayor was a kick. A fun old guy with a great sense of the ridiculous, he was the easiest authority figure Diego had ever worked with. Which meant he'd better get over it. Things that appealed in his life? They always ended up short-term, if they even lasted that long.

"Probably just making his decision to bring someone

in look good," Diego said dismissively with an uncomfortable shrug.

The teasing smile shifted to contemplation as Jade studied his face. Finally, just as he was about to actually shuffle his feet, she handed him his coffee.

"Applebaum really isn't into the spin game. I mean, there's not much point in a town this size. I think that's how he's gotten reelected so often. People know he's telling the truth," she said before gesturing toward the room behind him. Diego glanced at the plush, curvy couch. Bright blue, it was diamond-tucked with at least a hundred buttons, glossy wood accents and curlicue legs. It should have said fussy discomfort, but he could picture Jade laid out there in a sassy, sexy invitation much too easily.

He looked over her shoulder toward the dining room table with its long bench-style seats. The hardwood looked as if it'd make for some uncomfortable sexy times, not in the slightest bit encouraging toward stripping Jade's clothes off one piece at a time to search for invitations.

"Why don't we take this into the dining room." He covered his inward cringe with a big smile. "I was hoping for some cookies, and the table means fewer crumbs, right?"

The smile she flashed was bright and happy, as if he'd just answered the secret question and was about to be awarded his prize. Diego's heart picked up a beat as his imagination flipped through all the prizes he'd like from her. Most involved bare skin and a few required feathers.

"I figured you'd be cookied-out after all the offers this afternoon. But just in case..." She gestured toward the living room again. He followed the wave of her hand. A tall tree, glistening in rich jewel decorations, was displayed in the window. In front of the couch was a low table that looked like a polished brass surfboard. On it were some magazines, a free-form glass bowl in brilliant shades of streaky blue, indigo and purple, and an old-fashioned holiday tin with a bright red lid. He glanced back at Jade in question.

"The cookies are already out," she said. Then, taking matters into her own hands, she skirted around him. Not touching, not even close to making inappropriate contact. But the glance she offered through her lashes was as naughty as if she'd pressed her breasts into his chest. His body reacted as if she had, too, his breath catching and his dick going hard.

"It's comfier in here. And besides, if we have cookies here, Persephone will leave us alone. If we eat in the dining room, or even sit in there, she's going to raise a ruckus."

Diego gave the cat a doubtful look. It looked harmless. "A ruckus?"

"Yes," Jade confirmed, sinking onto the couch as if the matter was all settled. When she curled her feet up to tuck them beneath her hip, he figured in her mind, it actually was. "In here, she'll jump on the couch, check us out, then curl into a ball under the tree and nap. If we were in the dining room, she'd weave between our feet meowing, angry that she can't get up on the bench or table to dismiss what we're doing."

Bowing to the inevitable, Diego crossed the room. A quick glance told him that the other seating choices weren't optimal. One was a round footstool, about four feet in diameter and covered in furry leopard print. The other looked like a prop from a fifties movie, with its angular shape and retro polka-dot fabric. Safe enough to sit in, but made for a pixie-size woman. Reluctantly—at least that's what he told himself—Diego sat on the couch with Jade. As far away from her as he could get. So far, their body heat didn't even mingle. So far, he couldn't reach out and trail his palm over the smooth line of her jaw, or comb his fingers through those silky strands.

Close enough, he figured, that if he kept a cookie in one hand and the cup of hot coffee in the other, he'd do just fine.

"Here," Jade instructed, pulling the red lid off the cookie tin to show a variety of holiday treats. "Cookies fresh from my mom's kitchen. And that shoe-shaped disk? That's a coaster. Just set your coffee there."

He glared at the bright red shoe with its glittery bow and glossy heel. A coaster. A sexy coaster. What better to lure him into temptation with.

Stop, he silently demanded. He was here to solve a case and get the hell back to his own life and his bright new promotion. Not to be led around by his dick and quite possibly hurt what was probably the nicest, sweetest, sexiest woman he'd ever met.

"Have a cookie and tell me more about yourself, Diego," she invited with a smile warm enough to melt the frosting off the holly cookie she'd chosen. She bit off a piece, the crispy cookie snapping. Her tongue, small and pink, slid over her lower lip, gathering the scattered sugar.

His mouth watered. She'd missed one glistening green crystal. It sparkled, tasty and tempting, inviting him to lick it off the corner of her mouth.

"How about we talk about the case instead." He didn't care if he sounded desperate. He knew damn well that the minute his coffee cup met that shoe coaster, he was in a whole lot of trouble.

JADE'S LOWER LIP trembled a little. She didn't want to talk about the case. She didn't want to think about some panty-stealing creep being in her house. In her underwear. She didn't want to consider what it meant that the crimes had gone from undetected thefts to someone breaking in and trashing her bedroom. Either the creep was escalating to meaner crimes—or he had it in for her, specifically.

Instead, she'd rather take comfort from the information her mother had passed on. Apparently, Opal had been chatting with the mayor, who'd filled her in on Diego's many crime-fighting talents. The good detective had quite a fan in Applebaum. Of course, rumor was that the mayor was in talks with two neighboring towns to create a dedicated police force so they didn't have to rely on the county sheriff any longer. He'd gone on and on about Diego's close rates, his ability to think outside the box and what sounded like an almost mythical talent when it came to reading people.

Diego was here to solve this case. And she had complete faith that he'd do so—and keep her safe while he was here. But the minute he nabbed the Panty Thief, he'd grab his duffel bag, swing one long, lean leg over that big beast of a motorcycle he'd driven into town on and roar right back out.

As if to prove her point, he dug one hand into the pocket of his leather jacket and, still holding his coffee as if it was a lifeline, pulled out the little notebook he'd used all day.

She figured she could pout that the sexiest man alive was only here for a tiny amount of time, barely enough for her to learn his loner ways and independent spirit. Or she could make the most of what little time there was before he left.

"So you'll be heading back home soon," she said before he could start flipping through his notes. "Just in time for the holidays and all that, right? Do you have special plans?"

As in, a woman to kiss under the mistletoe? A family hell-bent on setting him up with Ms. Perfect? A slew of lovers waiting to unwrap his…package?

"Special plans for what?"

"Celebrating, of course. Tree-trimming parties, naughty-gift exchanges, secret-Santa festivities. You know, plans."

He looked so baffled, she had to force herself not to scootch over and give him a hug. It was as if he'd never experienced Christmas. At least, not a fun, festive one. The kind with candy canes and homemade decorations. Carols and cookies by the tree.

The kind she took for granted. Jade glanced at the cookie tin, feelings of guilt and joy mingling. Diablo Glen might not be the fashion mecca of the world, but it was pretty awesome in so many other ways.

"I'm sorry," she said, giving in to the need to touch him by patting his thigh—and what a strong, hard thigh it was. "But I think I'm going to have to expose you to as much Christmas as I can while you're here in town. I'm pretty sure it's my moral obligation."

"You have a moral obligation to foist tinsel and sugar cookies on people?" He sounded horrified.

Jade grinned. "Okay, it's my holiday obligation. And it's more than just sugar cookies, you know. There's gingerbread, too."

"That's okay." He gave an adamant shake of his head.

"No, no," she said dismissively, waving her hand as if he'd protested out of some need to not put her out rather than dread. "I really want to show you the delights of the season, and you can say a lot of things about Diablo Glen, but you can't claim we don't know how to show Santa a good time."

"You should save the good time for him, then. I'm fine without it."

"Nope," Jade insisted, both amused and delighted at his baffled reaction. "We have wonderful seasonal celebrations every day in December, winding up with my mom's open house on the twenty-third. Tonight the grade school chorus is doing a musical of *How the Grinch Stole Christmas,* the O'Malley family are doing hayrides through town after sunset and the ladies' auxiliary kicks off their annual sugarfest fundraiser."

Maybe it was his look of baffled trepidation. Or maybe it was the need to show him a little holiday cheer. Or, more likely, it was a desire to spend as much time as possible with him before he roared off into the sunset.

Whatever it was, Jade was determined that for whatever time he was here, Diego was going to experience a Diablo Glen Christmas.

"You'll have fun," she insisted, offering him another cookie from the tin. She wanted to see if he actually could have fun. Did being a loner who only had to answer to oneself mean giving up the simple, easy pleasures?

"I'm not interested in fun." He didn't sound sure, though. His eyes, hooded and intense, dropped to her breasts. Jade's breath caught. Her heart skipped a beat before racing like crazy through her chest. Her nipples stiffened, pebbling tight against the red lace of her camisole. Nerves raced faster than her pulse. She wanted him like crazy. She'd give anything to taste him, to strip him naked with her teeth, then run her tongue over his bare skin.

Her fingers trembled. The shaking was accompanied by a rattling sound. Realizing she was still holding out the tin of cookies, she lifted it a little in question. His eyes met hers again.

"Christmas is my favorite time of year. The lights, the glitter. All the great presents," she babbled nervously. "You really should give all the celebrational fun a try."

"Maybe next year," he said, making it sound like maybe never. She wanted to push, but the look on his face, closed and distant, said *back off.* Figuring she'd done enough to promote the season—for now—she complied.

"You're up for a promotion," she said with a smile, shifting topics and choosing a stained-glass sugar cookie for something to do with her mouth besides irritate him. "Will you still live in Fresno when you get it?"

"I'll be transferred to San Francisco."

"Oh, fun," she exclaimed, not a little envious. "I love it there. I used to live in the Haight, in the cutest Painted Lady. It was one of those gorgeous Victorians all done up in bright colors and divided into four condos. Walking distance to the best boutiques and oh, man, the food."

"You lived in San Francisco?"

Jade frowned. Why did he sound so shocked? Did he think she couldn't fit into such an exciting, metro place? That she was so small-town she couldn't handle the culture and diversity and challenge of one of the most dynamic cities in the world?

"I lived there for two years while I went to school at the Art Institute. My degree is in fashion merchandising and management." She tried to smile, hoping it'd take some of the stiffness out of her words. If the narrow look he gave her was any indication, it didn't come close.

She waited for the inevitable questions on why she'd returned to Diablo Glen. Whether she hadn't been able to hack it or if she'd come running back like a homesick small-town girl. Or if she'd been so overwhelmed by the expenses and the pressures and the demands, she'd used the first excuse she could find to throw it all away and scurry back to mommy.

Jade puffed out a breath. Maybe she had a few issues.

"I'm confused," Diego said after a few seconds. "Aren't you a librarian?"

Well, that hadn't been on the list of neurotic questions she'd been prepared to field. Feeling as though her skin had shrunk two sizes too tight, Jade wrinkled her nose.

"No. Absolutely not." Realizing she sounded as if he'd just accused her of skewering Santa with a metal nail file, she sucked in a breath and tried to tone it down. She really did love the library and respected the profession, so she tried to explain. "I mean, I work at the library, but that's not my vocation. I love clothes, love creating looks, but I don't have the imagination to be a designer. I *do* have a great eye for combining pieces that suit people, in bringing together a look, an outfit, a style."

Diego blinked a couple of times, as if he was trying to connect the dots, but a few too many were missing for him to make a solid picture.

"It was my dream, working in fashion." She tossed the uneaten cookie on the table with a sigh. "But family obligations, expectations, they got in the way. You know how it is, right?"

His eyes softer than she'd ever seen, he looked as if he was going to give her a comforting hug. Jade started to lean forward, more than ready to feel his arms around her. Then he shook his head.

"No. My only obligations are to the job."

"How do you avoid family ones?" she asked, wondering if she should take notes.

"No family. No obligations to avoid." His words were flat, his eyes cold.

"But..." Jade's words trailed off, her mind flailing about, searching for a way to put to words the millions of questions suddenly bombarding her mind.

"I have a mother, she's still alive. Somewhere," he said, his tone as distant and cold as the North Pole. He didn't drink his coffee to warm it up, though. Instead, he stared off at something only he could see over Jade's shoulder. "She was a party girl, only dropped into my life once or twice before heading off to the next thrill. Dumped me in foster care, or with an uncle now and then."

Jade pressed her fingers to her mouth to hold back her protest.

"It's no big deal," he said, seeing the look on her face. "I did fine. And it's easier to focus on the job without those obligations you talked about."

Jade's heart melted in sympathy, tears threatening, hot and burning in her eyes. That poor little boy. No mother, no family, no love? How'd he survive? What incredible strength did he have inside that had placed him on this side of the badge instead of the other?

"You're not getting any sloppy sentimental ideas over there, are you?" he asked, his tone as light as possible for someone who sounded as if he had his nuts in a vise— emotionally speaking, of course.

"Me?" she asked with a cheery laugh. Blinking fast to ensure her eyes were clear and bright, she picked the cookie up again and nibbled. The sugar tasted like dirt, gritty and bland. "Sentimental? Unless you're talking vintage fashion or stop-motion Christmas cartoons, I'm never sentimental."

She shifted on the couch, making her once-over look like a teasing inspection, when she was actually looking deeper, as if she could actually see the emotional scars.

It was easier to kiss them better if she could see them first.

"Look, it's no big deal. Lots of people grow up in worse situations. I had food, shelter, all the fundamentals. I turned out fine."

Indeed he had. Which spoke more to his inner strength than the resilience of human nature.

"You're disillusioned," she observed quietly, her heart weighing heavy in her chest as she traced a soft caress over the back of his hand for comfort.

He laughed, the sound surprised, not cynical. "Disillusioned? Nah. You have to have illusions for that, don't you? I never had any."

"What about being a cop? You had to have illusions of what that'd be. Is it what you expected?"

After a few seconds, he met her eyes again. The frustrated disappointment in his dark gaze made her feel as if she'd just kicked a sweet little puppy.

"Yeah, I guess I am disillusioned."

"Yet you do a job that requires that you believe in good," she marveled.

"Believe in good? Hardly. I deal in proof of the exact opposite." His bitter laugh wasn't an insult to her, she realized, her smile sliding into a frown. It was directed at himself.

"You believe in the power of justice. In right and wrong. And you believe, you must believe, that you can balance the two somehow," she said, her words soft, almost a whisper. As if saying it too loud would send him flying off her couch and out that door.

Still, she couldn't not say it. She spent most of her life keeping things in. Playing nice and not speaking out, worried about making others upset or uncomfortable. But unlike her family, with whom it would serve no purpose to share her dreams and frustrations, Diego needed to hear what she had to say.

Her fingers skimmed his wrist and forearm, muscled and tense. Hard. Like the rest of his body.

He needed to know what she felt.

She let her eyes travel from her fingers, milky white against his golden skin, up his deliciously muscled arm and broad shoulder to the curve of his chin. The soft, just-this-side-of-pretty fullness of his lower lip. The sharp line of his nose and—her breath caught as she met his gaze—the intensity of his dark eyes.

He should be told what she saw.

"You really are a hero, aren't you?"

He cringed. Beneath her fingers, his arm tensed. She figured he was mentally already halfway out the door.

"I like heroes," she murmured, risking his mental trip shifting into high gear and sending him running all the way out of town. She didn't care. She didn't know how he was key to her happiness, to her freedom. She just knew her gut believed it. Which meant she had to take the risk. Had to tell him her truth.

The horrified look in his eyes turned speculative. Hot. Sexy.

Jade slid her hand up his arm, sighing in appreciation as her palm skimmed the hard, round rock that were his biceps. She pressed her fingers to his chest. There, just between his heart and his shoulder. The heat of his skin through his T-shirt warmed her palm. Filled her with a desire strong enough to drown out the nerves clamoring through her body.

She stared into the rich depths of his eyes for a second, then let her gaze drop to his lips. Full, tempting lips. The hint of stubble. The small jagged scar above his mouth.

She wanted to taste them again. Needed to feel them against hers. He'd kissed her once and now it was an addiction. She had to know what else he could do. They'd done the hard-and-fast route. Could he do wild and intense? Was it in him to be slow and sweetly gentle?

Maybe it was time to grab on and enjoy finding out.

Hardly daring to breathe, Jade leaned forward. His eyes narrowed, a dangerous heat flaring in their hypnotic depths. Her stomach jittered.

Nerves racing with excitement, she shifted closer. Close

enough for the tips of her breasts to brush his chest. Her nipples instantly stiffened. Desire, hot and molten, ran down to her core. The intensity of it made her dizzy.

Just a simple touch and she was teetering on the edge of an orgasm. God knew what she'd do if they actually got naked. Melt into a puddle all over his bare toes?

She narrowed her eyes. And him? He still had that same stare going on. How did she entice a man so sexy he probably had women throwing themselves at him every day? How did she satisfy a man whose expression she couldn't even read?

The only way to find out was to try.

Even if it scared her to pieces.

She wet her lips. Then, eyes locked on his, she leaned in and brushed her mouth over his jaw. Soft and unthreatening.

His body was rock hard. His expression didn't shift. But his eyes? They were flaming hot now, filled with a passion that excited, terrified, empowered her.

"I really, really do like heroes," she whispered again.

Then, just to see what they'd both do, she ran her tongue over his lower lip, sucking the soft, tender flesh into her mouth.

9

OH, BABY. He tasted so good. Delicious and decadent, with a hint of coffee and a sweet layer of powdered sugar. She wanted more. She needed as much as she could get. But she forced herself to pull back. Holding her breath, her stomach tumbling with nerves and excitement, she waited to see what he'd do. Kiss her back? Get up and leave? Both options were a little scary.

He gave her another one of those deep, soul-inspecting stares. Her heart raced and the nerves outdid the excitement, knotting themselves into a tangle. She resisted the urge to squirm.

"This is a mistake," he said, his voice a low, husky rumble.

"Do you always avoid mistakes?" Breathless and seductive, her words were both curious, and, well, yes, a little bit of a challenge. Because she didn't care if it was a mistake or not. She just wanted to do it again.

He didn't answer.

Instead, he kissed her.

Hot.

Intense.

Wet and wild.

Jade moaned against his lips as they slid, silky soft, over her mouth. His teeth nipped softly, so that she parted her lips to gasp. Then his tongue swept in, swirling deep. Sweet and hard at the same time. Deliciously sweet, and, holy cow, so temptingly hard.

She grabbed on to his shoulders to keep from melting all over him. His hands swept up her jeans-clad thighs, making a soft scraping sound against the crisp cotton of her shirt before settling on her waist. Her breasts grew heavy, aching as she waited to see if his hands would go a little higher. Just a little, please.

Instead, he gently pulled his mouth from hers and waited. Her nerves spun out of control. She didn't know what he was waiting for, nor could she tell if he was anywhere near as affected by that kiss as she was.

"Wow," she breathed in a rush, unable to handle the lack of commentary any longer. "You really are good at that."

His lips twitched, but he stuck with the strong, sexy silence as he tightened his hands around her waist, then effortlessly lifted her onto his lap. Jade giggled, excitement making her feel light-headed. Before she'd even settled—or had a chance to appreciate the hard length of his erection against the back of her thigh—he took her mouth.

And drove her crazy. Tiny nibbling kisses. Big eating bites. His hands stayed at her waist, but his mouth worshipped her in a way that was sexier than anything Jade had ever felt in her life.

She wanted more.

She needed more.

She reached her fingers under the soft fabric of his shirt, intending to take more.

Diego had other plans, though. He shifted, his hand covering hers.

"We should stop," he groaned against her lips. Then,

proving he had way more willpower than she did, he released her mouth and moved back. Just enough to shift the intensity from high heat to medium simmer.

She closed her eyes and leaned her forehead against his chest, gratified to feel his harsh intake of breath and racing heart.

"Why?" She didn't want to stop. Not now, not yet. Not while the passion swirling through her senses was promising such a delicious and powerful result. But she kept her hands to herself. Because forcing her needs, her wants, on someone else? That just felt wrong.

"Because you're a nice girl and I'm not a nice guy. Because I'm leaving the second I solve this case. And because I have nothing to offer." His gaze dropped to her lips and heated. As if he was magnetically drawn, he leaned closer again. Then, forcing himself to stop, he tilted his head back to glare at the Christmas tree, taking in deep, controlled breaths.

Jade sighed.

He was right. He wasn't a nice guy. Which was one of the reasons he appealed to her so much. He was a guy who led the life he wanted, and was strong enough to accept and deal with the consequences but still go his own way.

And she wanted all that. Even if it was just for a few days, she wanted to experience that kind of inner strength. Even if it was secondhand.

"I think what you have to offer is mighty appealing," she told him. Even though it took all her nerve, she held his gaze as she pressed her palm into the hard planes of his chest, then let her fingers slide downward. Just to the rigid flatness of his belly. Her fingers itched to go lower. To encircle the stiff length of his erection pressing against her thighs.

Maybe he believed her, or maybe he was feeling the

same intense need she was. Either way, he gave a slow, contemplative nod. Excited anticipation raced through Jade's system.

"Just so you know, fraternizing with me might move you to Santa's naughty list," he warned, nuzzling his mouth against the sensitive curve of her throat.

"Naughty, hmm?"

"Babe, I'm as bad as they come." He leaned back. Just enough to give her an arch look. "And you'd be bad, too. If I got your clothes off, I predict you'd find yourself doing all kinds of naughty things. I expect you'd even teach me a thing or two, as well."

"Me?" she asked in her flirtiest tone.

"You've got some naughty inside," he promised, his tone as serious as the intense nod of assurance he offered.

He was so cute.

Her hands cupping the incredible breadth of his hard shoulders, Jade laughed in delight. She'd already accepted that he was gorgeous, sexy and dedicated. She considered it pretty awesome that his lips were magic and that his hands held the secrets to all physical pleasure. But now he was fun, too?

It was almost too much for a girl to handle.

At least, not without giving up a piece—and oh, please let it be a tiny piece that she could afford to lose—of her heart.

The cautious part of her mind—probably ruled by all that nice he'd mentioned—worried. What did she know about Diego?

Other than the fact that he was gorgeous and sweet, smart and funny. That he was a good, solid cop who believed in justice. That he'd had a horrible, lonely childhood and deserved to feel loved—even if it was only the physical kind of love.

Was she trying to talk herself out of sleeping with him? she wondered. Or trying to justify stripping him naked, slathering him in whipped cream and calling him dessert?

Confusion, and fear, overwhelmed the passion. She wanted him, unquestionably. And she didn't know what scared her more. Having him, and it not measuring up to her expectations. Or having him and finding out it was better than anything she'd ever imagined.

Both were terrifying, because both would hurt.

"I should refresh our coffee," she decided, jumping up from the couch. It didn't count as running away if she only went as far as the kitchen, right? "Did you want more coffee?"

She grabbed his mug, sloshing liquid over her knuckles. She was halfway across the room before she realized the brew was still hot. She stopped so fast, it sloshed again. She set the drink aside before it landed on her feet.

"What's the deal?" Diego asked, rising as well.

He stood so tall, so broad and strong. But not intimidating, she realized. As crazy as it sounded even to her, he felt safe. He felt tempting. He felt like her once-in-a-lifetime chance to be as naughty as he thought she could be. To live her life for herself, her own way. To experience living in the moment, on her own terms. Everything she said she wanted but was too afraid to actually do.

Just like Diego.

"Jade?" he prompted. "What's wrong?"

She met his gaze, letting all her fears, her worries and probably even her naked soul shine in her eyes. Licking her lips, she gave a helpless shrug.

"I'm a little worried," she confessed. Before he could ask what about, she used both hands to gesture toward him, then waved one in the general direction of her bedroom. "I want you. It's all I can think about. Getting naked, getting wild, doing all those naughty things you mentioned, then hitting the internet to find a few dozen more to try out."

She took a second to breathe deeply and assess his reaction. Not easy, since he'd frozen. Probably afraid if he moved, she'd jump him. Which just showed how smart he was.

"But I'm not sure it's a good idea," she continued, figuring she might as well confess it all. If he was going to run screaming into the night, he might as well be well fueled. "I'm too smart to fall for you. You're temporary. You're not a relationship kind of guy. You're a loner who likes his life the way he's made it."

She paused, realizing that those were a lot of the reasons she was attracted to him. He was all that, smart and temporary. A loner who wasn't looking for more than she could give.

"You're right," he agreed slowly, a dark frown creasing his brow as he shoved his hands into his pockets and rocked back on his heels. The look he gave her was pure speculation. As if he knew her doubts went deeper, but knew the doubts she had about those doubts were huge enough that a simple push would send her over the edge. He just had to decide which edge he wanted her toppling over. "This spark, this heat between us? It's a bad idea. Better ignored."

Well, there you go. Jade set the coffee cup on a side table so she could cross her arms over her chest without tossing coffee all over the place. See, he agreed. The two of them, together, not a good thing.

"It'd feel good, though," she mused aloud, staring at the Christmas tree as if the right answer would suddenly appear beneath the green boughs, gift-wrapped in glitter and foil. "It'd be incredible. I've never been this attracted to someone. It's like all my inhibitions packed their bags and are ready to leave the minute you touch me."

Diego's groan pulled her out of her dreamy reverie. Jade winced, then couldn't help but grin as he shoved both his hands through his hair.

"You're killing me," he decided, his face a study in frustration.

Because he wanted her that much, she realized. Not just sex with any woman. Not just a notch, or something to pass the time while he was stuck in town. He. Wanted. Her.

"I'd rather you taught me how to be as naughty as you are," she confessed, her words rushing over the tops of one another in her hurry to get them out. To hell with fears. This was what she wanted, wasn't it? A chance to live life to the fullest.

Well, there he was, ready to fill her up. Her breath stuck somewhere between her chest and her throat, Jade waited.

Too bad she wasn't sure what, exactly, she hoped would happen when the waiting was over.

HE'D BEEN RIGHT. She was trying to kill him. Diego stared at the sexy little pixie, her blond hair swirling around her shoulders like fairy floss. Those eyes were huge, and if her words hadn't been enough to send him over the edge, she'd added a cute little nibble of her bottom lip to the mix.

This was insane. He should walk out the door right now, stay the hell away from Jade while he wrapped up this case, then get out of town.

Instead, he took two steps forward, grabbed her by the arms and lifted her onto her tiptoes to meet his kiss.

She gasped. Then, with desperate hands, she shoved his jacket off his shoulders. Diego released his hold on her waist just long enough to let the leather drop from his hands.

His mouth devoured. Lips raced. Tongues danced.

Her fingers clutched the back of his shirt. He couldn't get enough of her. Wanted more.

Needed more.

Diego shoved his hands through her hair, the soft strands wrapping around his fingers. He tilted her head back farther, holding her captive as he ravaged her mouth with the same edgy, desperate need he wanted to take her body.

"I want you," he confessed against her lips. "Now, desperately, I need you."

Too desperately. Diego struggled, using every ounce of willpower to keep his body in check. *Slow it down, buddy. Don't scare her. Definitely don't hurt her.*

"You want me?" Jade asked in a throaty voice. "Then take me."

Willpower disintegrated. Frantic animal passion took over. Barely aware of his moves, finesse and skill gone along with his mind, Diego could only feel. Only touch.

His hands skimmed up her tiny waist, curving over the delicious soft curves of her breasts. Already hard for him, her nipples pressed into his palms as if they were coming home.

He scraped his fingers over the pebbled tips, reveling in their getting even harder. Just like his dick.

"Lose it," he demanded against her mouth. "All these clothes have to go."

Her breath as shaky as his knees, Jade pushed against his shoulders until he released her. Then, her eyes glowing with slumberous pleasure, she tilted her head toward the hall. "My room?"

"Strip first."

Surprise joined the pleasure on her face, but only for a second. Then she arched one brow and gave him a look of pure challenge.

Her eyes locked on his, Jade unbuckled the vivid red

belt and let it drop to the floor with a light thud. Then, her fingers swift and easy, she unbuttoned the front of her oversize blouse. It only took a shrug of her shoulders to send it fluttering down over the belt.

His body tense enough to explode, he stared as she skimmed her fingers over her torso until they reached the lacy red hem of her camisole. Slowly, so slow he swore he was going to cry if she didn't get naked soon, she lifted the fabric. Higher, so he could see the smooth pale skin of her belly.

Diego groaned as the light glinted off her navel ring. Then Jade pulled the fabric higher, over her head, and tossed it aside. His gaze locked on the perfect curves of her breasts cradled in raspberry lace, he was barely aware that she'd pushed her jeans free of her waist until she kicked them aside.

He ate her up with his eyes. Her panties were cut high on the thighs, a narrow raspberry-colored panel of satin surrounded by ruffled lace.

"You are so sexy," he breathed.

"I think you're just obsessed with my lingerie," she teased.

Noting how the lace created a scallop design, dipping deep between her breasts, Diego couldn't deny that.

"You do have some incredible lingerie," he agreed. Then he flashed her a dare-you grin. "Maybe you can give me a little fashion show later. Take me on a tour of my obsession?"

"Maybe," she agreed, giggling softly. "Did you know that a woman's lingerie is more about her identity, her vision of herself, than it is about sex? What she wears under her clothes is like her secret self."

"You mean this sexy lingerie isn't all a show for the guys?" he teased.

"Oh, no. Guys are too easy. Lingerie is for women. To feel sexy about themselves, to prove to other women that they really are sexy. To make their secret self happy playing dress-up."

"Your secret self is the sexiest thing I've ever seen," Diego decided, tracing his finger along the edge of her bra. Dipping it lower, he rubbed her nipple with the back of his fingernail.

"I'm glad you like it," Jade murmured as she slipped her hands beneath his shirt. She gave a low moan when she pressed her palms to his abs. Diego grinned. He might not have lingerie, but thanks to no social life and an at-home gym, he had some pretty tight abs.

Then her hand slipped lower. Cupped his rock-hard erection through his jeans.

Diego's grin faded. So did his thoughts. All he had left was sensation. And that was being commanded by the hand on his control lever.

Her hand squeezed. Barely aware of the sound of lace ripping, Diego tore her bra away. He filled his hands with her soft flesh, his mouth with the rosy tip of her pebbled nipple.

She gasped, her hand clenching. Diego almost came right there in his jeans. Needing her now. Desperate to bury himself in her delicious warmth, he grabbed the edge of her panties and tugged. She gave a delighted shudder, her fingers working his snap and zipper with the same clumsy, desperate impatience he was feeling.

"I'll replace it," he promised, shoving the tattered satin aside.

"Naked," she demanded before he could reach the treasure his fingers sought. She gave up her quest to get his zipper past the rock-hard pressure of his dick. Instead, she scraped her fingernails lightly up his belly beneath his shirt. "Naked, now."

"I like a woman who knows what she wants," Diego said, his words as choppy as his breath. He forced himself to release her, stepping backward to tear his clothes off. He didn't take his eyes off her. Nude now, her body was a work of art. Petite, delicate, all sexy cream with berry-tipped breasts and a golden thatch of hair that beckoned him home.

Diego barely remembered to grab a condom from his jeans before he tossed them across the room.

Before they hit the ground, he had his hands on her again. His mouth took hers. His fingers slid down, dipping into the hot, wet delight between her thighs.

He wasn't going to last. He couldn't, he wanted her so badly. Sheathing himself now, before he lost the awareness to do so, Diego pulled her tighter against his body.

His hands curved down her hips, grasping the soft flesh of her butt and squeezing. Jade gave a mewling sound. Then, her arms wrapped tight around his shoulders, she gave a little leap and wrapped her legs around his waist.

Diego groaned, not sure whether to be thrilled with the new position or upset that the shift put her breasts out of reach of his mouth.

"That way," Jade instructed, tilting her head. He followed the tilt, noted the hallway, and, gripping her butt a little tighter so she wouldn't hit the floor, headed that way.

Walking became a new, delicious form of torture. Every step slid the hard tip of his dick against her curls. Every step was a new lesson in sexual torture.

He barely got halfway down the hall.

"Can't make it," he declared, turning fast to press her body between his and the wall. Grabbing her feet, he angled her higher. Then plunged.

Jade cried out, her throat arched and her breath came in fast pants. Barely able to see through the haze of passion, Diego watched the flush climb her chest, up her throat, and coat her cheeks in a warm pink glow.

Her heels pressed against his butt, urging him to go deeper. To move faster. Her wish being his command, he did exactly that.

He plunged. She swirled. He pounded. She met him thrust for thrust. She might be little, but there was nothing fragile about the hellcat in his arms.

He shifted, just a little, to angle her higher. She gasped. Her back arched, bringing those yummy nipples back within tasting range. Unable—unwilling—to deny himself, Diego took one delicious morsel into his mouth and sucked.

Jade gave a keening sort of scream, her body so tense it felt as if she could snap in half. Then she ground herself against him, wet heat sucking him in deeper.

Ready to pass out, breathing heavily with no blood getting to his brain, Diego let go. He plunged, nailing her to the wall. Her fingernails dug into his shoulders. He plunged again. She cried out urgent pleas for him to go harder. Go faster.

He came.

Wave after wave after wave, the orgasm pounded out of him with an intensity he'd never felt before.

Barely aware, unable to stay upright, Diego slid to the floor. His arms wrapped tight around Jade, he took her right down with him.

IT MIGHT HAVE BEEN ten minutes, it might have been an hour. Jade didn't know how long it took for her to float back into her body.

So this was what love felt like. She shifted so her hips

weren't pressed so tight against the cool wood floor. Her emotions had taken on a rosy glow that only added to the incredible sensations still trembling through her so-satisfied-she-was-exhausted body.

"It's too fast," she mumbled, trying to lure her heart back to the same side.

Silly heart, what did it know? This had to be sexual infatuation. Her body and mind were totally gaga over him, so her emotions were trying to join the club. Which was just crazy. She couldn't fall in love this quickly.

"You're thinking too hard," Diego muttered, his face still buried in her neck. Anchoring one hand on either side of her shoulders, he pressed himself into a push-up to get a look at her face. Not wanting to meet his eyes while all the crazy thoughts were still dancing through her head, she focused on the sculpted muscles of his biceps.

"You're so strong. So hard," she murmured, grazing her palm over his arm and purring in appreciation.

As distractions went, it worked pretty well.

"Hard, hmm?" He gave her a wickedly naughty grin just before he kissed her again. His mouth was ravenous. He'd just come with a power that had almost broken down her hallway wall. But she could feel him stirring back to life against her still-trembling thigh.

"Trying to prove something?" she teased.

"Let's find out."

His mouth trailed down her throat, kissing, nibbling. Delighting her with tiny shivers of pleasure.

Yeah, Jade sighed as she shifted her head to give him better access as he scraped his teeth over her collarbone. She was in love with him. It was too fast. Too soon. Too complicated.

"Way, way too fast," she muttered just before her body arched in a shocked gasp of delight. He sucked her nipple into his mouth, swirling his tongue around the hard tip and sucking at the same time. Jade's thighs quivered.

Who cared about time, though? She'd known Eric for twelve years before they'd gotten engaged. Look how that had turned out. With her secretly grateful that he'd saved her from a life of mediocre sex.

"Did you say you wanted it fast?" he asked, his voice an erotic rumble against her belly.

Tunneling her fingers into his hair, Jade gave a helpless laugh. "I don't think I can go much faster."

He lifted his head, his eyes slumberous and heavy with fulfilled passion. Slowly, like watching a fire take spark, the wicked gleam grew, intensified.

Jade's own eyes widened. Her pulse tripped.

His fingers slid down her hip and over her still-trembling thigh.

"What are you doing?" she gasped.

"Seeing how fast you can go."

His whiskers scraped a delicious path over her belly as he slid lower. His fingers combed through her damp curls, parting her. Exposing her. Making her tremble.

"Go...? Where?" Here, there, anywhere. She'd go wherever he wanted, just as long as he kept doing these sweet things to her body. Then he shifted again, scraping her thighs with his jaw as he settled in to feast.

His tongue dipped, swirled, dipped again. Jade's gasps were pants now, her head thrown back in delight as the sensations pounded through her body at the speed of sound.

"Go over," he demanded, adding his fingers to the dance.

Unable to do anything else, Jade flew. Faster and faster, the sensations swirled. Deeper and more intense, the orgasm quaked through her. Her legs shook. Her heart pounded.

"Oh," she gasped, soaring along the crest of pleasure with a power she'd never felt in her life. "Oh, I love this."

Unaware of anything but what was going on inside her body, Jade tried to think. Tried to focus. But she couldn't. Like a storm-tossed ocean, she crashed. Wave upon wave, the orgasm just kept going.

Slowly, breathtakingly slowly, the waves smoothed, softened. As if she'd been drugged, her body sank into an exhausted state of barely-there awareness. She had a vague sense of Diego lifting her, carrying her to bed. When the cool pleasure of her own silk sheets slid against her back, she tried to surface.

But then he kissed her. And she dived under one more time.

10

"Hello, son."

Diego jumped. Actually jumped, like a strung-out meth fiend trying to lift a cop's wallet. Four days in this town and look at him. It was pathetic.

"Sir," he said, wiping his palms on his jeans and nodding to the mayor in greeting.

"You're here for the meeting?"

"I thought I'd take it in."

Diego glanced past the older man to the ornate arched opening to the town hall. For a small town, Diablo Glen was sure big on fancy architecture. It was also home to an extensive arts program that included music, dance and three gallery shows a year. It didn't boast its own police department or newspaper, but it was home to a famous on-line bakery. And it was peopled with a lot of characters, some a little more out there than others. Only one, though, was unforgettably sexy, overwhelmingly sweet and pretty much the biggest mistake of Diego's life.

"Thinking you'll find some clues during our discussion over what color to paint the park benches this spring and which band should play at the New Year's Eve Bash?"

Tension rippled across Diego's shoulder blades as he

shrugged. Better to focus on his failure to close this case than on Jade, he figured. With that in mind, he followed the mayor up the wide steps, waiting while the other man unlocked the ornate doors.

"I figure it can't hurt. From what I've heard, pretty much everyone shows up for these things. Maybe I'll catch a break."

"Don't be down on yourself, Sandoval. You're doing everything right."

"If I was doing everything right, I'd have solved the case," Diego pointed out as he followed Applebaum into the cavernous foyer. His tone was matter-of-fact, but the look Applebaum gave him made it clear his frustration was coming through.

"Do you think all cases can be solved just like that?" Applebaum asked with a snap of his fingers. "Or is there a natural progression to investigating?"

"It depends. A case like this one, where the perp appears to have gone underground, it's harder," Diego admitted. At Applebaum's arch look, he shoved his hands in his pockets, rocked back on his heels and considered the bigger question. "But yeah, I think there's a natural progression. Except it's never the same from case to case. Each one has to be looked at individually, and treated as priority. Big or small, a good cop never gets lazy and follows a checklist."

Which was why Kinnison's rules and protocols drove him nuts, Diego realized. The guy was all about the checklist.

"I like how you think," Applebaum said slowly, with a look that made Diego want to squirm. It was as if the old guy was peering into his soul. What the hell he thought he'd find there was the big question, though.

Trying to shrug off the compliment, Diego looked around the room.

A large blue spruce decorated the corner, beribboned packages spilling out from under its boughs. It looked as if there were enough gifts for every family in town. What was that like, that sense of inclusion, of being a part of something that considered everyone so special, they all deserved presents? Diego could count on one hand the number of Christmas gifts he'd gotten in his entire life. It must be the effects of Diablo Glen's familial warmth and close-knit community that were making him suddenly wish his name was on one of those shiny boxes.

"Do you think this case is different, being small-town, than one you'd face in the city?" Applebaum asked, pulling him back into focus.

"Yeah, but not in the way you'd think," Diego said. "Crime is crime. Human nature doesn't change according to zip code. But in the city, I'd have other cases to work on while I was chipping away for a break. Here, I'm spinning my wheels, looking like a failure and, no offense, sir, bored to death."

Applebaum flicked a switch that lit the far rooms with a warm glow, then led the way into the main hall. Rows of chairs stood in neat lines, with cushioned benches along the walls. At the front of the room was a raised dais, ten chairs at the rear behind the polished mahogany podium. Directly behind the podium was yet another Christmas tree, this one decorated with cookies of all shapes and sizes.

"Then your problem isn't failure, son. It's that you don't have enough to do." Clearly a man of action, Applebaum gestured to the closet labeled Storage. "Go ahead and set up the refreshment tables, why don't you."

Diego squinted. He was kidding, right? Busy unlocking more doors, then wheeling out sound equipment, the old mayor didn't look back. Maybe he wasn't kidding. Clueless as to how a refreshment table should be set up,

Diego squared his shoulders and dived into the supply closet, hauling out three folding tables. He and the mayor worked quickly, the companionable silence only broken by the mayor's occasional instruction.

"So how did things go with Jade?" Applebaum asked after a while. His expression hidden under the podium as he hooked up the sound system, he sounded curious but nothing more.

Large stainless-steel coffeepot in his arms, Diego froze. Had Jade told someone about their night together? Not even a night, he swiftly corrected. More like a few hours. Hours of passion, power, sexual nirvana and an afterglow of terror.

"Jade?" he asked with an inward cringe. Just how much gossip did this small town have on tap?

She'd used the *L* word. Oh, sure, she hadn't said she loved him, per se. But "love *this*" was close enough to scare the crap out of him. So much that he'd been halfway to the door under the guise of rescuing his leather jacket from the sleeping cat when he'd glanced back. Lying, naked and deliciously glowing, on the hall floor, Jade had offered a sultry smile and he'd been lost. He hadn't been able to resist scooping her up and carrying her into her bedroom for one more bout of pleasure. But the minute she'd fallen asleep, he'd sneaked out.

The only thing he was proud of was the fact that he'd managed to keep the cat, who'd somehow decided he was the next best thing to catnip, from following him out into the decoration-filled world.

"I figured she'd open doors for you around town. Everyone loves her. And why wouldn't they? The girl is a wonder," Applebaum continued, as if he hadn't noticed Diego's lack of response. "She stepped right up when her daddy died. Gave up her dreams, moved back to town to take care of her momma. Not that Opal needs taking care of, now. But Jade promised Chris, so that's what she did."

"Her dad died when she lived in San Francisco?" Diego confirmed. Skilled in the art of interviewing unwilling suspects, he knew how to make it sound as if he didn't care about the response.

"Yep. Moved back, got engaged, went to work at the library. That first year or so after Chris died, Opal was in a rough way. The MS kicked into high gear, and her grief was taking over." There was something in the mayor's voice that caught Diego's attention. A sadness, mingled with a lot of admiration. For Jade's mom? Interesting. Before Diego could wonder about it too much, Applebaum continued, "Jade? She kept Beryl in school, made it so Ruby could marry without guilt and guided her momma back to healthy living."

"Jade was engaged?" Yes, he knew Applebaum had said other words besides those. But the rest were just blahblahblah in his head, unheard over the ringing of that announcement. "What happened?"

Applebaum peered around the podium, his arch stare making Diego hunch his shoulders. So much for his covert interview skills.

"Eric was her high-school beau. They'd split when she moved, but drifted back together when Jade came home. They were due to marry about four Christmas Eves ago. A week before the ceremony, Eric got cold feet. Apparently he couldn't handle the responsibility."

The responsibility of marrying a gorgeous, sexy woman who was as sweet as she was smart? One who had a body that wouldn't quit, a personality so fun it practically glittered and a talent with her tongue that had made him want to weep in gratitude.

"Was the guy an idiot?"

Applebaum gave an appreciative smile. "Idiot, careless ass, too weak to do the right thing. They're all the same in this case. I suppose he figured he did the right thing by taking total responsibility. He decided he wanted out of Diablo Glen, but Jade's ties meant she couldn't, or wouldn't, go."

Diego focused on settling the coffeepot onto the middle of the table, then instead of moving the table away from the wall to plug in the cord, chose to crouch underneath it instead. All he needed was a few seconds to process that info. A moment or two—without Applebaum's eagle eye on him—to accept that Jade was here for good. Not that he'd thought about asking her to leave. Or considered what it would be like if she happened to move back to San Francisco after he was transferred there. It wasn't as if he'd already come up with five or six different options for asking her out. Nope. That she and Diablo Glen were permanently attached didn't matter to him at all.

Teeth clenched so tight his jaw ached, he rose, flicked the switch to make sure the coffeepot was juiced. Then, blank, he stared at the white table until Applebaum cleared his throat.

"Maybe grab the other coffeepot, and the big trays on the storage shelf?" the older man suggested gently. "I'd appreciate it."

Get a grip, Diego warned himself. And the speculative look in the mayor's eye served as a solid warning. Asking meant caring about the answer. And he had way too many reasons not to care. So instead, he asked, "So what's the deal? Does Jade's history have something to do with my case?"

Applebaum's face was tough to read. The speculation was still there, making Diego's shoulder blades itch. There was a weird, fatherly sort of benevolence in his eyes, and a shrewd tilt to his chin.

"Probably not. But it never hurts to have as many details about the people you're dealing with as possible."

Almost as confused by the paternal affection Applebaum treated him with as he was wondering about Jade, Diego decided that a mental-health break was mandatory.

"I'll be outside," he told the mayor. "Gotta check in with Kinnison, follow up on a few loose ends back in Fresno."

"Uh-huh."

Shoulders stiff, he took his time sauntering out of the room. No point in confirming that knowing look on the old man's face.

Forty minutes later, Diego deemed it safe enough to go back into the hall. He'd had enough time to check in with his boss, confirm that he'd be in court in January and give himself a nice long lecture on the need to live in the real world, how life in Podunk, Nowhere, was just fogging his brain and that sex was sex—not a golden ticket to the magical world of happiness.

Figuring he had himself lectured into shape, he stepped into the hall. And winced. It was like walking into the BART station when the train was pulling through. Crazy loud, he saw Applebaum hadn't been kidding when he said everyone came to these meetings.

This was it. His chance to get a solid lead and solve this damn case. Before he ran out of lecture material.

"Detective."

He returned the greeting with a nod. And the next one, and the ten after that. He turned down three offers to save him a seat, two plates of cookies and a chance to hold someone's baby.

Still shuddering at the last offer, he approached the refreshment table.

"Coffee, black," the woman behind the table said as she

handed him a large mug. "And I saved you a slice of gingerbread. Fresh this afternoon and still warm."

Nonplussed, he stared at the plate and mug for a second before taking them. "How'd you know—"

"Doesn't take more than two visits before I figure out someone's tastes," Lorna said with a big laugh that made her round belly jiggle. "Since you've eaten in my diner every night for the last week, I figure I've got yours down pat."

Not sure if that was a good thing, Diego muttered his thanks.

"Not that I'm trying to run business away," she continued, talking as she laid cookies out on plates, her hands as dark as the chocolate filling. "But there are plenty of people who'd be happy to have you to dinner. To show appreciation, you know. And, of course, to pump you for information."

Figured. Nine out of ten people who talked to Diego wanted something. Information on their case, something to fuel their gossip, dirty little secrets, tips on skirting the law. Or sometimes it was simple—they just wanted him to sign off on their traffic ticket.

"Appreciation for what?"

"Those obnoxious panty thefts have stopped since you came to town." Before Diego could deny credit for that, she continued, "As for information, well, you're the hottest catch in town, Detective. The married women want to know your romantic history and if you'd like to date their daughters, nieces or cute neighbor. The single women are wondering a whole lot more."

His jaw dropped.

Before he could figure out how to process that image, someone jostled his elbow.

"Oops, sorry, Detective. Lorna, give me one of those

snickerdoodles, please, before my boy gets here and tries to eat them all up."

Mind still reeling, he stared blankly at Marion Kroger. The librarian frowned back, then gestured to Lorna for more cookies. "Well, this can't be fun for you. I'll bet you want to get home to your family, start celebrating the holidays. Have you given up on finding the silly pranksters yet?"

Brow creased, he watched her take a plate, piled high with a dozen glistening cookies. "I'll be here until the case is solved," he said.

"Oh, dear," Lorna exclaimed. "Even through the holidays? Not that I don't admire a man doing his job, but this is the time for family. Can't you come back after the first of the year? I'm sure people will still have panties missing in January."

"Nope. No family, so no problem seeing the case through. I'll solve the case before January, no problem," Diego assured Lorna.

Marion and Lorna both stared. Then, dark color washing her cheeks, the diner owner cleared her throat. "So, Marion. I see you have more family visiting. A whole truckload, from the looks of it. Are they all here for the holidays? Or to help you harvest your Clementine crop?"

"Oh, a little of both," Marion said before eating two cookies in rapid succession. "I wish you'd share your recipe for these, Lorna. They're about the best in the world. Detective, have you tried one?"

His intuition was zinging, the tiny hairs on the back of his neck standing on end. Why? While his mind replayed the last few minutes, he automatically accepted the proffered cookie.

Before he could hone in on what'd flipped his intuition switch, or even take a bite of the cookie, there was a loud commotion by the door. Gasps and yells, the sound of chairs banging together, skidding across the floor.

Diego ran toward the back of the hall. Jade, Beryl and Neal all chased into the room after a streak of black fur.

Snorting, Diego took his alert system down a notch. This town had a crazy idea of just what constituted an emergency. His eyes locked on Jade, who resembled a fashionable butterfly. She looked totally out of place in her body-hugging sweater dress, the cherry-red knit hugging her slight curves from shoulder to knee. Paired with knee-high suede boots and a matching black vest, she looked totally rock-star-does-Christmas. Except he didn't figure too many rock stars entered a room crouched low to the ground, trying to catch a cat.

"I've got her," Neal yelled, sprinting toward the raised dais, leaping and damn near landing on the frantic feline. He landed on his knees. The cat launched itself into the tall Christmas tree, scurrying through the branches. As she got higher, Diego could see something dangling from her mouth. Eyes narrowed, he tried to make out what it was.

"Neal, be careful," Beryl pleaded breathlessly, bending low to rest her elbows on her knees and pant.

Apparently his idea of careful was to grab for the cat, who growled, gave a spine-shuddering howl and reached one paw out to take a swipe at him.

"You…" Face screwed into an expression of anger, his mouth tight with embarrassment, the younger man grabbed again. He missed the cat, but got hold of whatever was in her mouth. He yanked. Hissing, the cat yanked back. He pulled harder, making the whole tree lean ominously as onlookers yelped and cried out warnings.

"Don't hurt her," Jade yelped. "Just let her calm down. Then I can coax her out of the tree."

"You get her out now," Marion Kroger demanded.

"Those are real cookies hanging there. Food products. They can't come into contact with a dirty cat."

Diego slanted the woman an ironic look. "What? And after hanging a few weeks from a tree that spent most of its life outside, they're gonna be edible?"

"That's not the point," the librarian said gruffly, red washing over her cheeks as she glared at the cat, who was now mewling pathetically about a foot over Diego's head.

Neal pulled again, snagging the white fabric away from the cat. Her mouth now empty, she tried to take a bite out of his hand instead. Cussing, he shook a bough.

"Neal!" Jade yelled, shoving at him so he let go of the tree. He stumbled. His fingers caught the ribbon of a dangling gingerbread man and yanked the tree sideways so it tilted precariously. The cat hissed, giving him a slit-eyed growl that made the hair on the back of Diego's neck stand on end.

"Enough," he commanded. "Jade, calm down. I'll get your cat."

A cat that was now perched somewhere around the ten-foot mark in that tree. Diego looked around, then pulled the heavy podium forward. He couldn't get it close enough to the tree, though, because Neal was in the way.

"What're you doing?" the guy asked, scurrying out of the way at Diego's arch look. Diego didn't bother to answer.

"Be careful," Jade said. He smiled at her. A mistake, since she smiled back.

"Here, son," the mayor said, holding out a broom.

"He gonna swat the cat out of the tree?" Neal asked, laughing.

"Balance," Diego said, wondering if he'd been that stupid at twenty. Since Jade was looking as if she might shove him again, Diego figured he'd better get the cat fast, before he had to arrest her.

Great. Just what he needed before he did a balancing-act cat rescue in front of half the town. The vision of Jade, in handcuffs.

Naked.

JADE WATCHED, her hands clenched against her churning belly, as Diego effortlessly vaulted onto the tall podium. She should be too worried for Persephone to be turned on over the way his biceps flexed. Tell it to the tingles, she decided since she didn't seem to have any control over her body's reactions when it came to the sexy cop.

Two days of avoiding him hadn't impacted her reaction one bit. Nor had the endless lectures. The man might be off-limits and out of her league—although she could get used to a dozen orgasms a night pretty easily—but she still wanted him.

Good thing she lived in the "you don't always get what you want" world.

On the edge of the podium, teetering dangerously, Diego stretched his arm up toward Persephone. The cat gave him a long look. Then she let go of whatever she'd been hauling around in her mouth to issue the saddest, most pathetic meow Jade had ever heard out of her.

Sniffles and sad *awes* filled the room. Someone rubbed a supportive hand over Jade's shoulder. Recognizing her sister's touch, she reached up to take her hand.

"Be careful," she cautioned Diego again, this time in a whisper. As if thinking the same, the entire room had hushed. She didn't have to glance behind her to know they were all staring, breaths held, as if their tense waiting would keep Diego from falling.

As Diego stretched higher, Neal scurried forward to grab whatever Persephone had dropped.

"They're just doll panties," he said with a laugh, holding

up a pair of tiny cotton drawers with lace trim. "Looks like the cat probably dragged them off one of the Victorian carolers in front of the church. Guess we didn't need a fancy city cop to figure out who the Panty Thief is."

There was a scattering of laughter, but it died quickly. Jade was too afraid for Persephone to spare a glare to toss at Neal. But her growl elicited another shoulder pat from her sister. Whether Beryl's gesture was to keep the growl from growing into a threat or in sympathy, Jade didn't much care. She'd deal with the smart-ass who'd scared her cat up the tree later.

The fancy city cop was now standing on top of the podium, stretched dangerously high with one hand anchored on the broom handle the mayor held for balance. The other was lifted overhead, holding a small piece of cookie as bait for the terrified feline.

"Let's try for some quiet, please," the mayor requested, sounding his usual calm, controlled self. But his knuckles were white on the broom, a furrow of concern creasing his brow.

As usual, his loyal constituents fell in line, quieting the roar to a sibilant whisper punctuated by the occasional comment or cough. Jade, standing at the base of the dais, could now hear Diego's murmured encouragement.

"Aren't you the pretty kitty," he said softly, his words not carrying beyond Jade, Applebaum and the cat. "Did that dumb guy chase you? Aren't you uncomfortable up there? Bet you are. Come on down here. I'll give you a cookie."

As he soothed her cat, Jade finally tore her terrified gaze away from the hissing fur ball to look at Diego. His face was tense, his body pure muscled control. She recognized his cop mode, but beneath it was actual concern. For her cat.

Jade pressed her hand to her belly, promising herself

the sinking feeling there was worry. Nothing crazier than that. Diego Sandoval was inspiration, eye candy and entertainment. But that was it.

"This is stupid. Can't we start the meeting already? The cat will be there when we're through. Probably come down on her own if we get on with things, instead of standing around like a bunch of dorks watching some hotshot cop show off."

"Neal!" A loud smack accompanied the exclamation.

It could have been the sudden noise, or maybe Neal's obnoxious comments, but Persephone started. With a loud growl, she scurried even higher up the tree, now teetering precariously at the very top, her paws wrapped around the gold star. The bough, slender and green, bent sideways. Ornaments crashed to the floor in a loud, shattering clamor.

"See what you did."

"Smack him again, Beryl," Jade muttered as her sister's admonishment was echoed through the room.

"Just saying it's stupid," Neal said, sounding as if he was pouting. "The cat's safe. She climbs trees all the time. I figure she must be happy up there, surrounded by all those decorations and stuff."

Diego ignored it all. Hand still stretched so high Jade figured he must be getting a shoulder cramp, he continued to murmur sweet endearments.

Suddenly the cat jumped. With a loud, miserable-sounding moan, she launched herself from the star toward Diego. Jade ran forward. The mayor bobbled the broom. Gasps and warnings chorused around the room.

Other than letting go of the broom so he had both hands outstretched, Diego didn't move. Which meant he was right there, in bull's-eye position, when Persephone landed on his chest.

Jade's knees almost gave out. Tears sprang to her eyes,

relief pouring through her in a hot wave. Babbles, laughter, cries of relief all rang out. Bodies surrounded Jade, pushing her backward, farther away from the dais, her cat and her hero. On tiptoe, she could see Diego take someone's hand to get down from the podium. He kept the cat curled tight against his shoulder, though.

It took Jade a solid five minutes to make her way through the admiring throng. As soon as she was close enough, Jade's gaze raced over Diego, looking for scratches or punctures. He didn't appear to have a single one. Frowning, she shifted her look to the cat. Purring, Persephone's eyes were slatted, her tail curled around Diego's forearm and her paws resting comfortably on his chest.

She was safe. Unharmed. And so, so smug.

A gurgle of laughter, part relief and only slightly hysterical, escaped. Diego's eyes met hers.

"Thank you," she said, easing between a few more people so she could run her hand over the cat's silky fur.

"It was nothing."

Nothing? Neal had chased her cat through the streets, up a tree and Diego had saved her. That was hardly nothing.

Her mouth trembled. Her lips parted, just a bit, as she sighed. Then, forgetting that they had an audience, she stood on tiptoe and pressed a kiss to his cheek.

"You really are my hero," she whispered.

"I'm not anyone's hero. Never have been, never will be." His words were stiff, uncomfortable.

Maybe it was her ego talking, but to Jade, he sounded as if that fact might cause him a little bit of regret. Not enough that he'd bothered to call, though. Not that she cared. That's how things were in the big city. Itches got scratched, needs got met. All it added up to was a really good time.

"Don't try to tell my cat that," was all she said, though. Then she added, "I'm pretty sure she thinks you're her hero, too. Big-tree rescue, keeping the mob contained and stopping them from chasing her. And didn't I see you feeding her cookies? She's going to be yours for life now."

Diego ducked his head, making a show of glaring at the cat. Jade's lips twitched. He looked so cute when he was embarrassed. Whether it was the hero reference, or because he'd shown her multiple glimpses of heaven two nights ago, then spent the last couple of days trying to avoid her. Given the size of Diablo Glen, she'd been impressed with his success.

She supposed she should have been hurt, too. What girl wanted to be avoided like an STD after a hot, sexy night with a gorgeous guy? But she'd seen the fear on his face after the first time they'd made love on her hallway floor. And she'd seen the intense desire that'd replaced it. If she were a loner, hell-bent on going her own way without commitments or ties, she'd have left before sunup and played the avoidance game, too.

So what if she'd felt a little rejected when she'd woken up alone. And if she'd rolled over to tightly hug the pillow he'd slept on, it'd just been for a second. Just long enough to remind herself that he was her motivation. A role model to study, to figure out how to emulate so she could find a way out, too. What would that say about her if the instant she found someone who embodied everything she'd been wishing she herself could be, she started wishing he would change?

A heavy heart and empty bed? No big deal, she assured herself. To prove it, she gave Diego a friendly smile.

His frown deepened.

"Your cat is a menace," he told her, handing over the purring bundle of soft fur. "Do you always bring her to town meetings?"

Gathering Persephone close, Jade buried her nose in the

purring cat's fur for a second before giving her a fierce look. Despite cats' fabled ability to land on their feet, she'd been terrified that her beloved pet was going to end up a splat on the podium.

"I try not to let her out of the house from Thanksgiving to New Year's. I came straight from the library, but she was locked up safe and sound when I left this morning."

His frown shifted in an instant, going all cop.

"Someone was in your house? Let's go."

Still holding the cat close, Jade laid one hand on his forearm. He froze. Went rock-still. Was that a good thing or bad? Without permission, her gaze dropped to his jeans. Did her touch turn him rock solid everywhere?

"No," she finally said, after a quick squint in the murky light didn't tell her one way or another. "My aunt was in town and said she'd drop off some packages for me to wrap. She probably forgot to keep Persephone inside."

He nodded. He didn't relax, though. If anything, he tensed up even more. Because now it was just them, she realized as her stomach sank into the toes of her Frye boots. They weren't talking about the cat rescue, or the need for him to pull out his detective's badge.

Her breath stuck somewhere in her chest, Jade sucked in her lower lip and sighed.

"Wait," she said, her words low and husky. Quiet, because of the crowd encircling them. Afraid he'd think they were a come-on, she cleared her throat and tried again. "I mean, can we talk?"

He looked as if she'd asked him if he wanted to strip naked and climb back up the Christmas tree while singing "Grandma Got Run Over by a Reindeer."

"About the case," she said. If cop mode was all she could have from him, she'd take it. At least until he realized she wasn't trying to lure him into anything. Not a relationship, not a commitment. Not even her bed. "Or, you know, we can just sit and I'll protect you from all the matchmaking mommas who are eyeing you right now."

His cringe was infinitesimal, but she knew she'd hit her target when he cast a wary eye around the room.

"I'm not interested in matchmaking," he said loud enough to make a couple of matrons frown. Then he met her gaze, his dark eyes serious, with just a hint of regret. "Or in being matched."

Jade's expression didn't change as she slowly nodded. Message received.

"I'm not either. But we can be friends, can't we?" she asked quietly. Her heart trembled in her throat as she stared into his eyes, waiting for his response. Hoping it'd be positive. She might not get to keep him forever, or even for a little while. But couldn't she have him for just a little longer? Maybe just until Christmas, since he was her Christmas wish.

Because no matter how much her heart whined, she didn't expect him to change. She'd given up too many dreams for other people's good that the idea of someone giving up even a portion of theirs for her filled her with dread. Not even if it meant that he'd suddenly realized he was insanely wild about her, and declared his life incomplete unless she climbed on that Harley behind him to ride off into the sunset.

"Got a solid hold on your cat?" he asked.

Jade blinked in confusion, but checked her grip on Persephone. "Yes?"

"Let's go then."

"Go?"

"Go talk."

11

DIEGO STOOD in the doorway, waiting while Jade checked all the windows and doors in her house to make sure the cat's escape had been an aunt-related error and nothing else.

She'd invited him in, but as much as he hated looking like an idiot, he hadn't felt it smart to go farther than the entry. Not until they'd established a few things.

So there he stood, looking at anything and everything except his own personal crime scene, aka her couch. But not looking didn't stop the memories of how she'd looked, naked beneath him. Of how her skin had felt, silky soft and sleek under his hands. Of how she'd tasted, rich and tempting against his tongue. The sounds she'd made echoed through his mind like the sweetest song, one he was desperate to hear, again and again.

But as long as he didn't look at the couch, he'd be okay. Like looking into that snake-headed gal's eyes...avoid them and he wouldn't be turned to stone.

Trying not to feel like a wimp, Diego gratefully greeted Persephone as she padded out of the kitchen to wrap around his ankles.

"You doing better now?" he murmured.

She meowed and looked up expectantly.

For what? He'd done his good deed for the day. Unless she was about to splat against a hard surface again, this was as close as they were getting.

He crossed his arms and stared. She stared right back.

He wasn't about to be intimidated into submission by something that weighed less than ten pounds.

She stood on her back legs, leaning both front paws against his knee. Then, in evil-cat fashion, she rubbed the side of her face against his leg.

"Crap."

Glancing around to make sure Jade wasn't nearby, he held out his hands. The cat plopped back on her butt and glared.

"Best offer," he told her. "Take it or leave it."

With a graceful leap, she took it. He tried not to grin as she curled against his chest as she'd done earlier, purring like a freight train.

"Told ya you were her hero," Jade said.

Diego damn near tossed the rumbling cat across the room. He hadn't heard her come in.

Jade didn't smirk, though. Instead, she looked serious. Like a woman who wanted to have a talk. His gut tightened, but avoiding the couch was about as chicken as Diego would allow himself.

"I think she's still stressed from her tree adventure," he defended, handing Jade her cat, despite the feline's protest. "No reason to think I'm a hero for just doing my job."

Jade gave him a long look before bending down to set the cat on the floor with a quick scratch behind her ears.

"I suppose 'hero' is just a part of the job description for you," she commented as she straightened. The move shifted the knit fabric so it slid temptingly over her body, hugging her waist, curving along the sleek lines of her hips. "But Persephone and I aren't used to heroes, so we think it's pretty special."

He remembered what Applebaum had said about her fiancé bailing at the last minute. Compared to a loser like that, he could see why someone who did the right thing might seem heroic to her. Diego frowned. But that didn't make him one.

"Look, we need to talk."

"Hmm, I'm pretty sure I said that already." Her tone stayed serious, but her eyes danced with humor as she gave him an arch look.

He'd sneaked out of her bed like a creep, turning an incredible night of passion into a cheap one-night stand. He'd spent two days avoiding her and hadn't had the courtesy of even acknowledging what an ass he'd been. And she wasn't pissed? As he crossed his arms over his chest, his frown shifted into a glower. What the hell was she up to?

"Did you want to sit down?" she invited, waving a hand toward the living room. Diego's gaze inadvertently followed to land on the blue velvet couch. The soft, tempting blue velvet couch.

"No."

"You'd rather stand here, in the hallway?" She still sounded serious enough, but her lips were twitching now.

Why was she so easygoing? He'd spent enough time in Diablo Glen, talked to enough people and heard enough gossip to know that Jade Carson didn't have guys sliding in and out of her bed.

So why wasn't she more, well, girlie about it?

Unless she was relieved.

Diego's ego cringed.

"I'd rather say what I have to say," he told her quickly, needing to get back on track before he gave in to his ego's need to prove his worthiness. "After I'm through, we'll see what's what."

She bit her lip as if debating whether or not she wanted to hear him. He figured not. But like broccoli and exercise, it'd be good for her. And for him, he admitted with a sigh. He wasn't a fan of opening up and sharing. But he owed her.

"I need your help on this case," he admitted, figuring that was the best place to start. A factual appeal to her civic duty.

"Again, I'm pretty sure I've made that offer already." She stepped around him, close enough that the floral scent of her twisted through his senses. It wasn't perfume, he remembered. It was her shampoo. Soft, like roses at midnight, with just a hint of citrus. She didn't touch him, though. Just moved past and settled onto the bench next to the front door.

"You didn't want to sit," she explained, "but my feet are killing me. These boots weren't made for chasing a cat through town."

Diego just nodded. He didn't want to get distracted, afraid that the minute they shifted into comfortable, friendly chatter he'd forget why he'd agreed to talk.

"I need your help," he repeated. "But we need to establish some parameters."

"You want my help, and you want to make sure I agree to follow your rules before you let me give it?" she clarified, finally showing a crack in her friendly shell. Anger sparked, making her eyes flash like brilliant emeralds.

When she put it that way, his request sounded so arrogant. Then again, there was a good reason why he was a loner. He didn't do this talking crap very well.

"Look, I told you that I'm up for a promotion. Get-

ting it means a lot to me," he explained, biting back the
impatience and trying to sound reasonable. "But for that
to happen I have to stick tight to regulations on this case.
Sleeping with someone connected to the case falls in the
category of flipping off the spirit of the regulations, even
if it doesn't break the actual rules."

When her eyes rounded, he wondered if he'd gone too
far. Maybe he should have sugarcoated his comments? But
her complacent sweetness was digging at his ego.

"So sleeping with me was a bad career move? Is that
why you sneaked off without even a goodbye? The reason
you've avoided me the last two days? Because you're afraid
of upsetting your boss?"

He winced. When she put it that way, it sounded pretty
rotten. But, again, she didn't look hurt. Or pouty or upset
or about to throw a tantrum. None of the typical female
responses. He narrowed his eyes, suddenly more worried
than he'd have been if she'd hefted a big-ole frying pan
toward his head. Instead, she looked like a woman who'd
just grabbed the gauntlet. Not good.

Like a clever cat stalking a wily mouse, Jade stood. The
slow smile curving her lips was wicked. Wicked enough
to make him forget she was a good girl. To forget he didn't
do small towns, that he didn't do good girls and that he
wouldn't be around long enough to get his fill of her, even
if he forgot all the rest.

She took three steps forward, close enough for him
to feel her body heat. With no input from his brain at all,
his body leaned toward hers. He craved the feeling of her
soft warmth again. The memory of her breasts crushed
against his chest filled his mind. Sent the blood pounding
through him to energize—and harden—his entire system.
He craved the taste of her. He needed to touch her. He desperately wanted to strip her bare and worship every inch

of her before driving the hard, throbbing length of himself into her waiting heat.

Diego tried to swallow, but his mouth was too dry. At that moment if his promotion sprouted wings and flew around his head screaming warnings, he'd have swatted it away.

Then, with that innate instinct some women had, Jade seemed to realize that he'd hit his breaking point.

And she used that exact moment to lean in just a little closer. So the flowery-citrus scent of her shampoo filled his senses. So close he could see the creamy perfection of her skin and know for sure that her lush black lashes were a gift from Mother Nature, not Maybeline.

So close he could reach out with one bite and eat her up if he wanted.

And man, oh, man, he wanted.

The look in her eyes warned him that she'd bite right back. And there'd be nothing sensual about her move.

"Look, hotshot," she said, tapping her silver-tipped red fingernail against his chest three times. "I've already taken the ride, so I can say firsthand that you're amazing in bed. The key to hearing angels sing, even."

His ego purred.

"But?"

Because he knew there was a *but* there. One that would probably make him look like an ass.

"But I don't have to chase a man to get him into my bed. Nor do I have to trick him or trap him or play some silly game to keep him there…." Her pause was a work of art, drawn out just long enough to make it clear who she thought had played the game. Then she tilted her head to the side, so her hair swept like a silken wave over her shoulder. "And I promise, if we end up naked together again, it'll be because you begged me."

This time when her gaze swept his body, it was as electrifying as if she'd skimmed her fingers over his hard, bare flesh. Despite the cool air, a trickle of sweat slid down Diego's spine.

"And if that happens," she continued, her tone as arch as the look she gave him, "I promise, I won't be as easy on you as I was last time."

He couldn't help but be impressed. He'd never been put so tidily in his place. Even as his brain flashed danger signals, his bruised ego demanded a chance to prove itself. His body was aching to let it have its way. Begging was looking pretty damn good.

He was insanely attracted to her big eyes and the appeal of her dimples. Her body was a gorgeous combination of curves and sleek lines. And those legs. His mouth watered just thinking about how they'd felt wrapped around his hips. Throw in her taste in underwear and she was just about the sexiest woman he'd ever met.

But he was pretty sure it was her smart-ass mouth and clever mind that attracted him the most.

A scary thing for a man who prided himself on the fact that the few relationships he'd ever had were emotionally distant and completely superficial.

"I'd beg for you," he said, putting it all out there because she deserved nothing less. "But that'd be a mistake. A big one. For both of us."

Her eyes flashed hot and excited at his vow to beg, then dimmed as she frowned.

"A mistake? We were pretty freaking awesome together." The crease in her brow deepened as she tilted her head to the side. "Weren't we?"

"Yeah. We were. But I'm short-term. As soon as I solve this case, I'm leaving," he reminded her. If nothing else, he had to know he'd been honest. He might not be able to give her hearts and flowers and forever. But he could give her honesty. Well, honesty and the most incredible sex she'd ever had. Except he shouldn't be thinking about the incredible sex, he reminded his hardening body. He shouldn't be angling to have it again and again and again.

But he was.

"You're going to do your best to solve the case as fast as possible. Which means you'd feel guilty, like you were doing a hit-and-run, if we kept getting naked together," she stated. No recriminations, no pouting. Just simple understanding. Diego swore, if he believed in love, he'd have fallen for her right then and there. The woman was incredible.

As if she'd read his thoughts and figured it was time to step up the game and show him a whole lot of you-ain't-seen-nothing-yet, Jade offered a slow, sexy smile.

"You really are a hero, aren't you?"

"I am not," he snapped, offended. Not offended enough to blunt his desire for her, though. Maybe if she insulted his manhood or disused Harleys, his hard-on would ebb.

"Sure you are. You're worried about me. You want me, but you need to do the right thing. So instead of begging like you'd like, you're going to push this—" she waved her fingers between their bodies, as if indicating invisible, yet potent, flames of desire "—away and pretend it's not flaming between us. Sort of like you sneaked out of my bed the other day."

He opened his mouth to deny sneaking, then snapped it shut and gave a bad-tempered shrug instead.

"You don't want a purely sexual relationship," he told her, even though he hoped he was wrong.

"Nope," she agreed. "I don't."

Diego nodded. See. He'd been right. It felt like getting kicked in the nuts, then force-fed liver and onions. But hey, right was right, even if it felt like crap.

"But I wouldn't mind an honest, open sexual relationship with a gorgeous man," she mused out loud. Her words were light and easy. The look in her eyes was intense and searching. "A friendship, hanging out together, maybe a few dates. No promises, no regrets."

"A relationship?" he hazarded, not sure since he'd never really had one. Didn't they come with requirements, though? Like no guaranteed expiration date.

"A relationship," she agreed, biting her lip and looking afraid for a second. Then she took a deep breath, as if gathering her courage. And gave him a smile that sent every concern, every argument, clear out of his head.

"Just like that?" he asked, realizing that feeling in his chest was hope. Almost afraid to believe, he gently settled his fingers on the slender curve of her hips. She felt so good, he silently groaned, giving in to the need to pull her closer. To feel her body, warm and soft, against his.

"Just like that."

His eyes locked on hers, he slowly—so, so slowly—lowered his head to hers. A second before he could kiss her, she pulled back a tiny bit.

"Except for one thing," she said.

Just one? He could think of a million things he'd do, offer, promise, to have her.

"Anything," he promised, meaning it.

"Say please," she whispered against his lips, her eyes lit up with wicked glee. Then she ran her tongue, hot and wet, over his lower lip.

"Please," he groaned just before taking her mouth with desperate, biting kisses.

Begging, his mind intoned. It does a body good.

How could a fully clothed, nonsexual encounter have her just as hot and bothered as a totally naked, decadently sensual exploration? Jade wondered. A week of hot, wild sex should have blunted her need for Diego, shouldn't it? Or at least put a dent in the clawing desperation to lick his hard...muscles.

Sitting on her living room floor, carols playing softly in the background as the tree lights flashed gentle colors, Jade was surrounded by wrapping, ribbons and glitter. All of which usually made her very happy. Dressing up a package was almost as fun as dressing up a person. At least, it usually was.

Today? She was so distracted, she'd wrapped Mayor Applebaum's cherry pipe box in Valentine's paper with a green bow before she'd realized what she was doing.

All she could think of was Diego. If she wasn't reveling in the incredibly erotic feel of the hard length of him inside her, or of how good it felt to slide down his body, curl her fingers into the scattering of hair across his chest and hold on while he took her for another wild ride, she was reliving it in her head.

She'd known when she'd invited him to continue their sexual relationship that she'd been asking for trouble. Sexy trouble, to be sure. But trouble all the same. But she'd figured it'd be worth it.

What she hadn't known—couldn't have expected— was to find out she liked him. Just flat-out liked spending time with him, talking to him, laughing together. They'd spent the last few days becoming, well, friends. He'd decided to lull the Panty Thief into complacency while still keeping a close eye on things. So they'd attended the high school's performance of Scrooge and the kindergarten recital of *The Nutcracker*. They'd gone to dinner, met Beryl and Neal for coffee, run into her mother and the mayor at the high school movie showing of *Grinch* and hit every boutique sale the senior ladies of Diablo Glen had to offer.

She'd loved every second of it.

And so, she suspected, had Diego.

And that was the scary thing.

"You're out of cat treats," he told her, coming into the living room. Having spent the past morning in Fresno testifying in court, he was dressed more formally than she'd seen him before. Black slacks and a black dress shirt gave him a dangerous air, especially when combined with the gun holstered at the back of his waist.

"A can of treats usually lasts her three months," Jade pointed out as she carefully measured a length of paper against a big box. "Someone has been spoiling her."

Diego's grin flashed as he settled into the wicker rocker. "I don't have to spoil her. She likes me." As if to prove his point, the cat padded out of the kitchen, still licking what was probably treat crumbs off her whiskers. She jumped onto Diego's knee, sniffed at the cup of coffee in his hand, then curled into a purring ball in his lap.

He arched a brow and grinned. "See."

Despite her dismissive eye roll, Jade was touched.

"So what's the deal?" he asked all of a sudden. "Did someone post a sign claiming my lack of family? Suddenly, everyone's trying to mother me. Or offering fatherly advice. Or worse, wanting to be my big brother or little sister. It's the weirdest thing I've ever experienced."

"I think it's sweet," Jade said, tucking her heels under her hips and rocking from side to side to settle into the pillow before pulling a large box toward her. "You know, for a guy who was so dismissive of small towns when you got here a week and a half ago, you're sure fitting in well."

"Just acclimating to build trust and break the case," he said dismissively.

Not an easy thing to do, given that after Persephone had been caught with the doll panties six days ago, most everyone in town figured her for the Panty Thief. Except the mayor, who refused to consider the case closed and set Diego free. Since Diego didn't believe that, either—after all, how many cats trashed bedrooms?—he hadn't argued much.

But Jade knew he was frustrated.

"Is that why I saw you working on Marion Kroger's car the other day?" she asked, teasing him out of the bad mood she could see him teetering on.

"Her engine wouldn't start," he said, staring into his coffee cup instead of meeting her amused gaze. "She had a trunkful of groceries that would have gone bad if she'd waited for a tow truck."

"I heard you followed her home, just to make sure she was safe."

He squirmed. Big bad cop squirmed. Jade pressed her lips tight to keep from giggling.

"Nobody likes melted ice cream at Christmas," he muttered. Then he gave her a questioning look. "She's got a lot of property out there, though. I didn't realize how big her orchards were. How does she handle all that, with just her and Neal to work it?"

"It is big, isn't it? I don't know how she does it, but she's making great money. Enough that she offered to buy Neal and Beryl a house as a wedding gift."

"Here?"

Wouldn't that have been nice? Jade swallowed the bitterness that coated her throat. A house, here in Diablo Glen, would have set Jade free.

"No. Neal wants to head down south. I guess it's always been his dream to live somewhere warmer."

Diego gave her a long look. Leaning over to set his cup on the table, he irritated the cat, who jumped off his lap.

With a growl and a glare, Persephone stalked over to the tree and curled up there.

"Why aren't you chasing your own dreams?" he asked, his words short, verging on angry. As if her being stuck here was a problem for him somehow.

"I have a life here."

"Not the one you want."

Jade focused all her attention on getting the bright red ribbon tugged and pulled so all the loops were even. It was hard to see them through the teary haze in her eyes, though.

"It's the life I've built, though," she finally said when she was sure her expression was serene. Meeting his dark, troubled gaze, she smiled. "Hey, I'm doing great. I have a secure job that, thanks to my grandmother leaving me this cottage, pays well enough to keep me in designer shoes. I have a wonderful family close by. A growing reputation as an It Stylist on the internet, thanks to Polypore. I'm even teaching a class at the college after the first of the year."

Deciding the bow was good enough, she snipped the ribbon at an angle, then tugged the ends into place before clapping her hands together to indicate a job well done.

"It sounds like a pretty good life to me," she insisted.

"But is it the life you want to be leading?" Without being asked, he hefted the now-decorated box and carried it to the tree, then grabbed another and set it in front of her to wrap.

Could he be any more perfect? He knew her needs, met them, without her saying a word. Just being with him made her happier than she'd ever imagined feeling. Her heart ached at the idea of what life would be like when he left. And he was worried that she wasn't leading the life she wanted?

Jade's smile hurt, but she didn't let it slip. Why should she? He cared enough to be angry for her. The least she could do was fake it enough to soothe that anger.

"Diego, sometimes it doesn't matter how good you are, how nice. Santa just can't bring you what you want." Which was why it was better to just not ask. It hurt less that way. "Unless you want to be miserable, it's smarter to figure out how to turn that lump of coal in your stocking into a diamond."

Or at least a chunk of prettily cut glass.

"I think it's crap."

Jade laughed.

"Seriously. You should be in San Francisco. Los Angeles. Hell, New York." He didn't sound very enthusiastic about that last one, though. "Somewhere that you could shine."

"I'm shiny enough here. Shinier, in fact, since I don't have much competition." Jade ran the strings of the gift tag through her fingers, twisting and untwisting the ends until the twine frayed. Finally, she gave a little shrug and met his angry gaze. "I can't leave. I thought I might, someday. But I can't."

He leaned forward, his shoulders hunched as if preparing to argue. Then he paused and looked closer at her face. Jade tensed. She hated confrontations. Someone's feelings always got hurt. And it didn't seem to matter if it was hers or the other person's, either way she felt horrible.

As usual, though, Diego surprised her. Instead of pushing the topic, all he said was, "Sometimes you need to put yourself first, Jade. People who love you? They'll understand."

Jade twirled the silver curling ribbon around her finger, then unwired it again. He was right. They would understand. But if she left to chase her dreams, someone else would have to give up theirs.

"And sometimes you learn to be grateful for the little things. Love means understanding why someone needs to leave, and letting them do it," she said, looking up to stare into the hypnotic depths of his eyes and baring her soul. "And every once in a while, it means being okay with giving up the dream so the people you love can have theirs."

If that wasn't enough to make a girl want to haul on the Grinch costume, she didn't know what was. Because her heart felt three times too big for her chest. He made her want more. Made her wish she could just grab on and demand more.

From her life.

From herself.

And from him.

12

DIEGO FONDLY REMEMBERED a time, not so long ago, when he'd known what to expect from life. People sucked, he could only count on himself and black clouds were the norm.

Ah, those were the good old days.

Now? Here in Diablo Glen?

Friendly residents acted as if he was one of their own, trying to include him in all sorts of cheerful holiday happenings. He'd lost his pen the other day and five people offered theirs. The last time he'd stepped into the diner, two customers had offered to buy his coffee. And despite the chilly December weather, it seemed like sunshine was the rule of the day.

It was freaky.

Freakier still was that he was starting to like it. Sort of. Or, he admitted as he dismounted his Harley, maybe that had something to do with Jade. What was with her? It was as if she was coated with some invisible magnetic substance. No matter how much he told himself to pull away, he couldn't. She was sexy. She was sweet. She was fun and clever and smart.

She was the woman he hadn't realized he'd been dreaming of. And now that he'd found her? Letting her go was going to be worse than being kicked out of every foster home he'd lived in, worse than watching his mother's back as she left him yet again. Because unlike the people who'd bounced in and out of his childhood, Jade was the real deal.

He was walking a tightrope already with his feelings. Her sweetness, her sass and her lingerie had all hooked him good. But the explosive power between them in bed had reached inside, to a place he hadn't even realized was there, and grabbed hold. He was terrified that if he wasn't careful, the minute he slid inside her again, he'd grab hold and never let her go. Drag her to San Francisco with him, promising her anything to get her to go.

Because she was so deeply rooted in this little town, taking her with him would require handcuffs, his sidearm and enough Christmas cookies to put her into a sugar coma.

And she'd still come back.

Shoulders hunched against that depressing reality, and not sure what to expect from Applebaum's summons, Diego stepped through the diner door. He looked around in surprise. A quick head-count estimate put the room at over thirty people. What? Every family in town had a body here for lunch? And what did it say about him that he recognized all of them?

Except the Hispanic couple in the far booth, he realized, narrowing his gaze and trying to place them. Definitely not from around here. He wondered if their car had broken down. They had the look of people who'd traveled a long way by foot.

"Hey, Detective," Carly greeted, a menu in one hand, her tray in the other. The pretty little redhead looked as if she should be in home ec. class instead of working tables. But Diego knew she was a mother of two, and if rumor was right, would have another stocking on the mantel next year. "The mayor's waiting for you at the back table."

The back table meant walking through the diner-filled sea of staring patrons. But unlike most places he was used to walking through, the stares weren't angry or hostile. They weren't coldly assessing. They were welcoming, most with cheerful greetings and a couple of friendly waves. Some were a little too friendly. He subtly shifted away from the table full of lunching moms all staring at his jeans as if their eyes were measuring tapes.

"The mayor's having the lunch special," Carly offered over her shoulder. "I can bring you the same. Or Lorna's got some of that corned beef you like. She'd be happy to make you a Reuben. Just let me know."

Debating, Diego glanced at the menu board. A one-pound meat-stuffed Asiago roll with a side of frings? Maybe he should find out who was next-in-charge in case Applebaum had a heart attack from eating that sucker.

"The Rueben sounds good," he decided.

They reached the booth set to the far back of the diner, at least five empty tables away from anyone else. Before he'd settled his butt on the soft fabric, Carly was back with a cup of coffee.

"You've got a strange town here," Diego said after the waitress had left to fill their order. "A whole bunch of people got their underwear stolen, the thief is still at large, and they don't seem to care."

"The thefts have stopped," Applebaum pointed out.

"The thief hasn't been."

"And that's bothering you?"

Diego looked at the older man as if he'd lost a few marbles. "Of course it is. I'm a cop. I was hauled here to solve a crime."

Applebaum sipped his coffee, watching Diego over the edge with narrowed eyes. "You're pissed."

"I didn't say that."

"Okay. Frustrated, irritated, stymied." He took another sip, but before Diego could find that tact he'd been warned he'd need, the mayor continued. "You're trying to figure out why I won't just cut you loose, since the crime—such as it is—seems to have hit a dead end."

"Your side job as a fortune-teller must come in handy come election time," Diego said, wondering why he wasn't more irritated. Everything the old man said was true. He should be stressed and anxious, furious to get done with this and get on with his promotion, his move and his life.

Except getting on with any of that started with saying goodbye to Jade. Diego stared into the murky liquid of his cup and sighed. Life had been better when he hadn't cared. It'd hurt less, and he was pretty sure his spine had been stronger.

"Why are you keeping me here?" he finally asked. Both to avoid the other points, and because he was actually curious.

Applebaum gave a low hum, then gestured with his cup.

"You see a lot of the ugly side of life in your line of work."

In his work. In his life. Same difference.

Something to remember. Definitely not the kind of life he should be wishing Jade wanted to check out.

"I guess I do. Crime's usually committed by ugly people."

"I guess it'd be hard to shift views, then. To see the good in people. See the possibilities and understand the motivation behind the foibles."

Diego had never had a guiding figure in his life. No dad to pass down wisdom. No counselor to motivate and inspire. So it was weird to suddenly find himself looking up to an older man, wishing he could embody some of the guy's wisdom. Wanting, just a little, to ask for advice.

Stupid. Applebaum was practically a stranger. One Diego would be saying goodbye to as soon as possible.

Diego cleared his throat, his gaze dropping to the smooth varnish on the wooden table. Time to change the subject.

"I have to say that you have a disturbing lack of perverts in this town," he said after a second. And he was truly bothered by that. Dirty old men, degenerates and moralless lowlifes were his stock-in-trade. But if there were any in Diablo Glen, they hid it well. Not just well enough to slide past his radar, but so well that they'd fooled the entire town.

"We have our share of characters. But most people looking for that kind of thrill have to go outside town to find dirt and kink. Still…" The mayor paused, giving Diego a long, searching look. Resisting the urge to squirm, Diego consciously cleared his mind of any and all kinky thoughts as they related to Jade. Which took him a couple of seconds.

"Still," the mayor continued, "we are seeing crime rise. Unlike the last decade, when more people moved away than were born here. Now the town is growing. Young families, kids who couldn't find jobs—or those thrills—in the city stay here, plus a few relatives who are looking for a nice place to retire."

Diego had watched enough baseball to recognize a windup. He wasn't sure where it was going, though. So he leaned back in the cushioned seat, waiting for the pitch.

"The neighboring towns are seeing the same thing. Between us, Barkerville and Middleton, we've seen our populations grow by a quarter in the last two years. There's no sign of that slowing down." Applebaum paused to take a deep, appreciative gulp of coffee, staring at Diego the whole time. Looking for what? "Given that, we're strongly considering not renewing our contract with the county for protection and starting our own police department instead."

Kerthud. His heart gave one strong slam against his chest. Possibilities swirled. None had anything to do with his personal career goals or ambitions. All had to do with what he was feeling for Jade. How had this happened? After a week and a half together, he was thinking about a future? Wondering how to mesh his job and her commitment to her hometown?

He had to force himself not to leap from the booth and race right out of town.

Just to prove he could.

"Me? I'm getting older. Not so old I can't take good care of Diablo Glen. But I'm starting to think there's more to life than the job," Applebaum mused aloud, staring out the window for a second. Then, as if snapping out of a reverie, he gave Diego an unreadable look. "I might be shifting a little of my focus, and I could use someone here in town that I can count on."

Someone was keeping secrets, Diego realized with a narrow look of his own. And keeping them damn well, since they hadn't surfaced on the town gossip wires. Curiosity, once only inspired by crime, flared in Diego's mind. What was the good mayor up to? Or should that be who?

"We just finished up the nail-down-the-details stages, me and the other two mayors," Applebaum said quickly, as if realizing he'd let on too much. "We're ready to start considering who we want as the chief of police. I think we'd be interested in chatting with you, boy."

As far as distractions went, that was aces.

Chatting. Diego resisted the urge to run his finger around the collar of his T-shirt to feel for noose fibers.

He was saved from responding by the waitress, who carried a tray much too huge for two sandwiches. The smile he gave her was so grateful, she blinked a couple of times before turning a soft shade of pink.

Then she swung the tray off her shoulder. Diego stared in shock. His sandwich was flat as a pancake compared to the mayor's.

"Is that a serving platter?" he asked as the waitress set the oval dish in front of Applebaum.

"That, my boy, is a delight to the senses." While the waitress unloaded her tray and refilled their coffee, Applebaum waxed poetic about his lunch choice. A strategic master, the mayor had cast out the bait. Now he was patiently waiting to see if Diego bit. And scarfing down the world's largest sandwich at the same time. The old guy was good at multitasking.

He'd be a good man to work for, Diego mused.

Shit. Appetite gone, Diego had to force himself to lift his tiny-looking sandwich to his mouth.

He might as well admit it. As much as he wanted to solve this case, snag his promotion and get the hell out of this tiny claustrophobic town… He didn't want to leave Jade.

"JADE?"

Jade set lacy cookies on a white doily, carefully widening the circle of sweet treats as if one millimeter of difference from one to the next would ruin her mother's annual holiday open house.

Since the gift-wrapping discussion two days before, she'd been avoiding Diego. In part because she felt as if he'd turned on her. No longer the sexiest adventure she'd ever had, he'd become a reminder of everything she didn't have. Which would soon include him and his incredible body, dammit.

"Jade?"

Why was he still here? She slammed the empty plastic container on the counter with the others, then grabbed a full one to start setting out fudge. Why didn't he call the case done, like everyone else had, and go? Just go.

What'd started out as a fun way to experience freedom and a little fun now felt like a prison. A tempting, orgasm-inducing prison.

It was enough to make a girl want to cry. Or—Jade shifted to ease the discomfort the waistband of her jeans were causing as they dug into her side—cause her to eat way too much chocolate.

"Jade!"

She jumped, and the fudge flew from her fingers to stick against her mother's kitchen wall with a dull thud. Jade's chocolate-covered fingers were halfway to her heart before she remembered she was wearing white.

"What?" she exclaimed breathlessly. "Why are you two yelling at me?"

Ruby and Beryl exchanged looks, with the eldest sister shaking her head and the youngest frowning with irritation.

"I've been calling your name for the last two minutes," Ruby said as she wiped her hands on a tea towel before stepping around the island toward Jade. "What's wrong?"

"Nothing."

Ruby arched both brows before tucking the towel into the waistband of her clearly not-too-tight skirt. For the first time, Jade wondered if her sister's perfect size three was due to regular married sex and a non-Diablo Glen zip code.

"Something is wrong," Ruby insisted. Then, ever the big sister, she shifted her gaze to Beryl, who was arranging cheese on a tray and wearing her own frown. "With both of you. What's the deal? I've been toting the good-humor banner all by myself this morning. Why are you two such grumps?"

"We're not grumps," Jade said in chorus with Beryl. She shared a smile with her younger sister, then realized that Ruby might be right. At least, as far as Beryl was concerned. The younger girl had dark circles under eyes that looked a little swollen. "Beryl? What's up?"

"Just like you said. Nothing."

Using Ruby's tea towel, Jade wiped the chocolate off her fingers, then off the wall. And debated. She knew her problem—kissing a dream goodbye combined with sexual frustration. But Beryl looked, well, sad. But the sisterly law of fairness said that if she wanted to prod her sibling, she had to offer up her own woes in exchange.

"See," Jade said as she turned to face Ruby, all the pieces of the fudge cleaned up. "We're fine."

Ruby split her irritated look between the two of them, then gave a jerk of her shoulder. "Fine? Be pouty and grumpy. See if I care."

"Since you're bossy, pouty and grumpy were the only T-shirts left," Jade quipped as she returned to arranging candy on her mother's favorite two-tiered Waterford server.

"Good thing they fit so well, then," Ruby groused. She glared at her sisters for a couple more seconds, as if her angry frown could scare confessions out of them. Then she threw both hands in the air and returned to the turkey she'd been slicing.

Adding peppermint fudge to the chocolate, Jade forced her expression to stay cheerful. She wasn't surprised that it actually hurt her face.

Not nearly as good at faking happy—why should she be, when Jade was the big faker in the family?—Beryl sniffled.

"Okay, that's enough," Ruby snapped. "I want to know what the hell is going on. You'd better just tell me now because I won't quit nagging until you do. You aren't ruining Mom's party with these crappy moods."

"Beryl, what's wrong?" Jade asked, setting the finished candy dish on the counter before moving to her little sister's side. "Sweetie, you're so unhappy."

All it took was an arm around her slender shoulders to turn Beryl into a crying puddle of mush. She clutched her sister, making Jade wince as her fingers dug into the delicate crochet of her knee-length vest.

"Neal and I had a fight," she sobbed into Jade's neck. "That's all we do lately. Fight."

"What are you arguing about?"

"He wants to move away. He's obsessed with going south, somewhere by San Diego or El Centro. His mom hates me—she must because she won't let me come out to their house. He is snappy and moody all the time—" she paused to suck in a breath, then before either of her sisters could say anything, she finished in a sob "—and I think he's cheating on me."

Jade blinked a few times, trying to process the laundry list of fighting topics. She gave their older sister a questioning look. Engaged couples fought all the time, didn't they? Well, she and Eric hadn't, but she didn't think they were the stellar example of a successfully engaged couple. Not when marriage was the final test, at least. So she didn't know. Were these normal reasons? Ruby's frown said this was something to worry about, though.

Her stomach tumbled at the concern on her sister's face. She pulled Beryl into a tighter hug.

"Why do you have to move away?" Ruby asked, tackling the easiest issue first as she rubbed Beryl's knee. "You love Diablo Glen. Both of you have family here, there are jobs and the real estate is more reasonable here than in most of California."

"He wants somewhere else. South, closer to Mexico. I still have a semester left of college and I kinda wanted to stay here for a while. Just, you know, to give it a chance before trying something else."

For one second—admittedly a bitter-tasting second— Jade wondered what it was like to have that sort of freedom. To only worry about what you wanted to do, where you wanted to be. Then, like dirty laundry and ugly shoes, she hid the thought away where she didn't have to see it, think about it or admit to having it.

"There's nothing wrong with staying here when you're through with school. Just for a while, to try it out," Ruby said.

"If you want to stay, tell him," Jade suggested. "You're building a life together, which means you get equal say. Don't give up what you want without a fight."

There it went, Jade's mental fraud meter, dinging out of control again. She really needed to live the life she preached one of these days.

"What if he says no?"

"Then maybe he isn't the guy for you," Jade said gently, giving her sister's hand a sympathetic squeeze. "But if he loves you, he's going to listen. He's going to understand why you want to stay here."

"Do you really think so?" Beryl asked with a flutter of wet lashes.

"Of course, sweetie," Ruby assured, giving her a tight hug.

"Heck, if you were staying for a while, you could have my place while you decided," Jade muttered. Her eyes rounded when, at her sisters' stares, she realized she'd said that aloud.

"Where would you live?" Ruby asked.

"Somewhere. Maybe somewhere else, you know." Jade

shrugged. Excitement spun in circles in her tummy at the idea of time, even just a little bit, to spread her wings again. Only this time, instead of seeing herself clubbing and making her fashion mark in a big city, she was cuddled up on a couch looking out a window at the cityscape, Diego's arms holding her close.

Pain, sharp and jagged, cut through her. Since when had he replaced her dream of happiness? And how stupid was she to have not stopped her heart before it got this close to danger.

"What's the deal?" Beryl pulled back to get a better look at her sister's face. "Is it that sexy cop? Is he why you'd give up your house?"

"I wouldn't give anything up for a man," Jade exclaimed. Well, anything besides her heart, her panties, her body, her dreams. All that minor stuff.

"You love your house," Beryl said, shaking her head. "I couldn't take it."

Knowing Beryl would guilt herself into moving out of town rather than take the cottage and inconvenience her, Jade rushed to say, "Maybe I could try something else. You know, somewhere else."

As soon as the words were out she bit her lip, as if she should pull them back in.

Ruby exchanged a long look with Beryl this time. Both sisters settled their butts more firmly in their chairs, as if gearing up for battle. Both folded their hands together on the tabletop and, damn them, both gave Jade identical knowing looks.

"You want to leave." Ruby made it a statement, not a question. "Why haven't you said something before?"

Tracing an invisible design on the hardwood with her fingertip, Jade stared at the table instead of answering.

"She did say something about checking into jobs in San

Francisco. Wasn't it last spring that you mentioned it?" her little sister asked.

Jade's shoulder twitched.

"And then I got engaged and said I was moving out of town," Beryl realized.

"And you figured you had to stay for good. Be here to take care of Mom," Ruby realized.

"You both had other stuff going on," Jade said, trying to make it sound as if it didn't really matter one way or the other.

"Saint Jade, always sacrificing." Ruby sighed, her tone somewhere between exasperated and angry.

"You both have lives outside town," Jade defended, irritated that her, yes, sacrifice was so unappreciated. "You've got a job and a life and Berry's got school and a future to build. I had, what? An underpaid internship and a ton of student loans. It makes sense for me to stay here." Sweet girl that she was, Beryl nodded. Ruby just rolled her eyes.

"Do you think Mom would want you giving up your dreams? Because, what?" she asked, the exasperation gone and anger taking full hold. "You have to babysit her?"

"I'm not babysitting," Jade snapped. Then, leaning forward so far her butt left the chair, she glared at her sister. "And don't you dare say anything to her."

Ruby shifted, too, so their glares were nose-to-nose. Before she could respond, though, the doorbell chimed. As one, the sisters winced and glanced at the cookie-shaped clock above the stove.

"Guests." With one last shake of her head, Ruby rose and gave Jade a narrow look. "We're not through with this."

"She's mad at herself," Beryl pointed out quietly as Ruby swept from the room. "You know Ruby. If someone's going to score the major sacrifice points, she wants it to be her." Jade's laugh was weak. So were her knees, because she knew damn well Ruby would follow through with her threat. They'd be having that talk, and as far as confrontations went, Jade figured it was going to be an ugly one.

"But just so you know, as soon as she's through with the sacrifice lecture, I want all the details on you and the hottie cop," Beryl said. It was clear from her tone that she knew she was adding punishment on top of punishment. It was just as clear from her smile that she was enjoying the idea.

Jade almost growled.

"Darlings," Opal said as she wheeled into the kitchen, her bright red scooter decorated with holly and pine boughs, her face so bright and cheerful she looked like a three-wheeled Christmas decoration. "People are arriving and you've spent enough time in the kitchen. Now, join me so we can celebrate the holidays."

Grateful for an excuse to run away, even if just for a few hours, from the box of worms they'd opened, Jade leaped to her feet and gathered as much food as she could hold to carry it into the dining room.

The Carson Family Open House was in its twentieth year, and the girls all knew the drill. Greet everyone and make sure they had food. Socialize with everyone and make sure they had more food. Keep everyone chatting with everyone else, and, again, make sure they had food. Opal Carson had a moral objection to anyone leaving her party anything less than stuffed till they groaned.

The sisters went their separate ways, and for once Jade was grateful for her mom's divide-and-conquer hostessing rule. She was kept busy enough to avoid even looking at her sisters. But there weren't enough people in all Diablo Glen to keep her from glancing toward the door every few minutes, hoping Diego would walk through. She'd invited him. Opal had invited him. She'd even heard the mayor invite him. Two hours into the party, she glanced at her watch. Shouldn't he be here by now?

"Did you hear the latest?" Mrs. Green asked, stubbornly standing with her crackers and cheese instead of sitting comfortably. "Applebaum got the go-ahead on the local police department. He and his crony mayors really did it."

"I'd heard that rumor." Almost a dozen people at the party alone had mentioned it. It was gossip, yes, but Jade knew most had said it as encouragement. Her seeing Diego was hardly a secret and they were all trying to make her feel better, as if there was a chance he'd stay. She knew better, though.

"Your pretty detective should take the job. He'd be good at it. He's got that strong, silent thing going on, like Clint Eastwood. But he's got a sweet side. Everyone likes him. More important, they respect him."

"He's fitting in really well," Jade agreed. Her face hurt from keeping the smile in place. It was like Eric's desertion all over again, only this time everyone was offering preemptive support. They were doing it to show they cared, but she really wished they'd stop reminding her of what she didn't—couldn't—have.

"I'd like it if he stayed around," the woman decided in her creaky voice. She inspected a pepper cracker from all sides before scooping up some cheese dip and giving Jade a wink. "He's got a nice butt. Strong, but pattable. That's what you want in a man."

Strong, but pattable? Jade's stiff smile melted into a delighted laugh.

"You're a treasure, Mrs. Green." She hugged the elderly woman carefully, so glad to have this kind of support. These kind of people in her life.

"Jade, we're running low on snickerdoodles," Ruby said quietly, offering Mrs. Green a friendly smile. "I've got to get more ice from the garage. Could you check the cookie trays?"

Jade gave the front door a hopeful glance, then deflated. She'd clearly used up all her holiday wishes, because it wasn't Diego who came in, but Neal and Marion.

She looked around for Beryl, sure her sister would greet them. But Beryl stayed in the corner, talking to a group of her girlfriends and their families. Brows arched, a little irked that she was now on greeting duty and a quest for snickerdoodles, Jade hurried to the door.

"Happy holidays," she said, her words as cheery as her smile was fake. Marion had been getting more and more irksome lately, and now that Neal had upset Beryl, Jade's mind was compiling lists of reasons why he was a jerk. "I'm glad you could make it. Let me take your coats."

"Your cat isn't here, is it?" Neal asked, looking around nervously. "I swear, it's got it in for me. All that growling and hissing and stuff."

"She's home, locked up safe and sound," Jade assured him as she draped his denim jacket over her arm.

"I'm surprised they haven't done something about her," Marion said, sliding out of her coat. Jade's brows rose as she took the rich, buttery-soft leather. The quilted design was gorgeous. Brand new, too. Oranges must be paying well this year.

"Who are 'they' and why should anything be done about my cat?" Jade asked as she turned to take their jackets to the small room designated as coat check.

"She's a menace. Neal already proved she's the problem behind the stolen underwear. Maybe they should put her down or something," Marion said contemplatively. "Isn't that what they do with dogs who've gone bad?"

Frozen in place by that horrible image, Jade's jaw clenched

almost as tightly as her fists. "Persephone hasn't done any-thing wrong."

"She's caused stress and drama all through town," Mar-ion countered.

Jade wanted to point out that Marion had done plenty of that herself. But the woman was a guest in her mother's house. Which meant it was time to get away before Jade said something her mother would make her regret.

"Help yourselves to the buffet," she snapped.

Forgetting the snickerdoodles, Jade tossed their jack-ets on the bench, not bothering to hang them up. Not even the gorgeous leather, which spoke to how angry she was. Needing air, needing space, she bypassed the kitchen and headed for the backyard. Blinded by anger, she made it all the way across the wraparound porch that encircled the house before she stopped short.

What the hell?

She blinked.

Then, ignoring her party makeup, she rubbed her eyes and blinked again.

"Mom?" she breathed.

There, seated at the old picnic table with her mother, was the mayor. His graying hair gleamed in the winter sun-shine. She couldn't see his expression, though. Because his face was plastered up against her mother's.

Her mom? And Mayor Applebaum?

Since when? And how? And, oh, God, why?

Baffled, too freaked to even want any of those ques-tions answered, Jade hurried around the porch toward the side, then the front of the house. *Home* was all she could think. There were snickerdoodles there. She'd bring them back after she'd sifted through the emotional hurricane of the last ten minutes. She figured it was a good sign when she reached the front of the porch undetected. Then her eyes landed on the eight-foot-tall blow-up Santa globe on the lawn.

She dropped to her butt on the top step and dug her fingers into her scalp, then lifted her head again.

Yep. Those were her panties, a bright red thong with glittery accents. In true holiday fashion, they were draped over the white fluffy ball of Santa's hat. Too high for her to reach. But in clear view, like a naughty beacon, for all to see.

Just when she thought the day couldn't suck any more, it proved her wrong.

13

DIEGO PULLED UP in front of the Carson house and dismounted the Harley. He squinted at Santa, then shifted his gaze to Jade. Then looked back at Santa.

"Those are yours?" he confirmed.

Jade cast a quick glance at the houseful of people, including, he imagined, her entire family. Then, with a wince, she nodded. "Can you get them without anybody noticing?"

"Sure." Diego reached into his pocket and pulled out his handy-dandy multipurpose knife. Before he could flip the blade, Jade rushed forward with a gasp and grabbed his arm.

"You can't stab Santa."

He grinned at the horrified look in her big green eyes. Unable to help himself, he leaned down and brushed a soft kiss over her open lips. She tasted like cinnamon. And now she looked shocked instead of horrified. Mission accomplished.

"Don't you trust me?" he asked, only half teasing.

Her eyes still a little foggy with desire, she shifted her gaze from his face to the jolly elf, then back again. Then she glanced over his shoulder at her mother's house.

"Just be fast." Her hand lingering on his arm for a second, smoothing over his bare wrist in the softest of caresses, she finally stepped back. "And quiet, too. He's likely to go out with a bang."

Diego grinned. Then, walking around her, he grabbed a low branch of the mulberry tree and cut off a long twig. One eye on the house, he reached up, snagged the thong on the end of the wood and flipped it into his hand.

"Quiet enough?"

"Perfect," she said, giving him a thumbs-up. Then she held her hand out for the panties. Diego, still inspecting her face, shook his head and tucked them into his pocket.

"You're upset," he observed.

"My panties were on Santa's head."

He noted the shadows in her eyes and the tension in her shoulders. His gaze slid to the house, full of people and obligations and expectations.

"Let's go," he said. Then, despite his vow to keep a physical distance, he wrapped his arm around her slender shoulders to guide her away from the house.

"I…"

"You should listen to me." He glanced at her feet. As expected, she wore skyscraper heels. White booties, they went just past her ankles to show off scrunched socks that glittered with silver threads. Skinny white jeans hugged her legs all the way to her hips, where her silky blouse was cinched with a wide silver belt. Fluttering ruffled sleeves and a vest that flowed from shoulder to knee completed the festive winter look.

"You up for a ride on my bike?"

Staring at him so hard, so deeply, he wondered if she'd delved into the secrets of his soul, Jade finally nodded. "Sure. A ride, a walk, whatever you'd like."

Diego almost groaned as a visual of all the things he'd

like flashed through his mind, most involving her naked, and one terrifyingly including old age, holding hands and scary commitments.

He handed her his helmet, watching to make sure she buckled up properly before swinging his leg over the seat. Then, even though he only planned on going a block or so, he took off his jacket and handed it to her.

"It gets cold on the bike," he muttered sheepishly.

"You are such a hero." Her smile was a little wobbly, but she pulled the black leather jacket on.

"C'mon," he instructed. Before his good sense took over and he changed his mind.

After one last guilty look toward the house, she complied.

How she balanced in those boots was a mystery, but she swung her leg over the seat, then slid close behind him. He wondered if she'd be willing to try it again, naked except for the footwear.

"Hold tight."

He kicked the bike to life, waited until her grip on his belly felt solid, and with her knees pressing into the sides of his hips, he roared off.

She waited until they got to the end of the block before letting out a whoop of delight. Diego laughed, feeling freer, happier than he ever remembered. Since most of the town was at the Carson open house, the streets were empty as he cruised around. He actually felt the tension draining out of her as Jade leaned into his back, her face resting against his shoulder blade. Not ready to end it, he took a side road out of town.

Opening the throttle, he roared away from Diablo Glen. The space between houses widened, serene green fields and orchards blurring as they flew by. When he came to a fork, he slowed. It was so tempting to keep going. But running wasn't going to solve anything.

As he turned back, the orange orchard in the distance caught his eye. He narrowed his gaze. The shadows of a dozen or more people moved between trees. Harvesting? Wasn't this a weird time to do that?

"Whose place is that?" he yelled over the engine rumble.

He almost regretted asking when Jade lifted her head off his shoulder. A chill shivered through him at the loss of her warmth.

"That's the Kroger property. I guess Marion's family is helping harvest this year. I don't know why she didn't bring them to the party, though. That's kind of rude."

She tensed up again, all the way back to the fingers digging into his abs. Brilliant detective that he was, Diego figured Marion had played a part in Jade's afternoon stress. Let it go, he decided. With one last glance at the orchard, he shifted into gear, waited for her arms to tighten again, then took off without asking any of the questions running through his mind. Five minutes later, he pulled up in front of her cottage. He smiled at the deep sigh she gave before she unwrapped her arms from his body.

"That was great," she said as she found her balance on the sidewalk next to him and took the helmet off. She ran her fingers through her hair, the pale blond glistening in the sunlight. "Thanks for the ride."

He took the helmet, debating whether to hook it to the seat or put it on and get the hell out of here.

"You're freezing," she realized, rubbing her hands over his arms. The warmth of her palms, the friction of her touch, sent a shot of desire right through his body. Diego shifted uncomfortably on the bike seat. Harleys weren't made for horny times. "Come inside. I'll warm you up."

He went rock-hard, making straddling the leather seat torture. His fingers tightened on the helmet straps.

"Hot cocoa? Maybe some gingerbread?" she tempted.

He should go. The more distance between him and Jade, the easier it would be when he left town. His detective's intuition was humming, the answer to the case buzzing just out of reach. He just needed a little time to mull it over. Distraction-free time.

"I have homemade whipped cream. It's great on warm gingerbread."

He swung off the bike and followed her up the steps like a lovesick puppy.

Freaking pathetic.

"I left my purse at my mom's," she said when they reached the door. Before he could offer to break in, she hurried back down the steps and around the side of the house. A few seconds later, she was back, key in hand.

"Who knows you stash a key?" he asked, frowning.

Opening the door carefully to make sure the cat didn't escape, she shrugged. She bent down, giving him a sweet rear view, and scooped Persephone up, then let the door swing wide to welcome Diego in.

The cat gave a long meow, leaped from Jade's arms into his. Diego laughed as he was hit in the face by silky fur. He met Jade's eyes over the purring mass. Her face was lit brighter than her Christmas tree. Every cliché of day's-end comfort, from a cool drink to a cute puppy with slippers clenched in its teeth, filled Diego's mind. None could hold a candle to feeling welcomed, feeling wanted, for the first time in his life.

JADE WISHED she could read minds. She'd give anything to know what was going on in Diego's head. He looked sad, confused and sexy all at the same time. The sexy she was getting used to. But big, bad, hotshot detective rarely showed any emotions, so the sad and confused worried her.

"Do you want whipped cream on your cocoa as well as your gingerbread?" was all she said, though.

"Sure." He gave her a long look, then smiled. "Whipped cream sounds good."

He followed her into the kitchen, where she started the coffee and pulled out a pan of gingerbread from the fridge. She set it in the oven on low to warm, then wordlessly gathered the makings of whipped cream.

Getting nervous at his continued silence, she took off his jacket so she didn't get anything on it. He tossed it over the back of a chair, then set the cat on the floor and took a seat.

"I heard you were at the Caroling in the Park this morning," she said, pouring cream into the freezer bowl she usually used to make ice cream. She added some sugar, a little vanilla and a splash of rum. "Did you have a good time?"

"Sure. It's a nice park. From what people were saying, you hold a lot of events there."

"Next to the town hall, it's the most popular gathering place." Over the sound of the hand mixer, she said, "You should see it in the spring. Flowers cover the gazebo, the barbecues pop up and picnics are the norm. The ladies' auxiliary funded new playground equipment last year, too. The swings are fabulous."

"I don't think I've ever been on a swing," he mused aloud, his attention on the cat, who was staring intently at his jacket.

"Never?" Too shocked to pay attention, Jade splattered not-yet-whipped cream all over the counter. With a grimace, she went back to aiming the mixer with one hand while wiping the mess with a towel in the other. Still, she eyed Diego. "I didn't realize it was possible to grow up without playing on a swing."

"Most of my trips to a park involve narcs, stakeouts or arrests." His words were offhand, his focus still on the cat, who was now growling at his jacket, swatting the pocket with her paw.

"You didn't have a lot of trips to the playground as a child?"

"I bounced around a lot as a kid. Foster homes, mostly in areas where playing in the park meant risking your life. Every once in a while, I'd be tossed back to my uncle. He lived in a Podunk town that wasn't big on strange kids." Diego's smile flashed.

If that wasn't a good reason to hate and avoid small towns, Jade didn't know what was.

She gave an obligatory smile, even as her heart broke a little. She'd thought it was so exciting, being a loner and not having to answer to anyone. But that meant not having anyone, too. *Loner* and *lonely* were the same, she realized. She wished she could wrap her arms around Diego and hug him close, so he felt loved, and never alone again.

Before she could figure out what to do with that realization, Persephone lunged with a hissing yowl onto Diego's jacket. Jade flipped the switch and tossed the mixer on the counter, running across the room to yank her cat's claws from the nice leather.

"I'm so sorry," she gasped, pulling back in shock when Persephone aimed a hiss her way. "I don't know what her problem is. She adores you."

A frown creasing his brow, Diego crouched down, holding out one hand. Eyes narrowed, the angry feline backed away. Jade gaped. The cat worshipped him. Why was she acting so crazy? Diego didn't seem offended, though. He was calm. Mellow, even.

The way he had when the cat was stuck up a tree, he murmured quiet nonsense talk. This time it didn't soothe or calm her, though. Instead, Persephone's paws shot out, snagging his jacket again. She hissed. Moving slowly, cautiously, Diego slipped his fingers into the pocket. He pulled out the pair of panties he'd stashed there after rescuing them from Santa's head.

The cat hissed again, gave an ugly growl and leaped at them. Snatching them out of his hand with her teeth, she flew from the room.

"Holy cow," Jade breathed. "She's never been like that before."

Diego didn't respond. He stared intently at the doorway through which the cat, and her bounty, had disappeared. Jade recognized his cop look, distant and considering.

"Diego?" she asked quietly, not sure what was going on.

After another second, he pulled his gaze back to her and offered a quick smile. "Well, that was fun. So, is the whipped cream ready?"

Jade studied his face, then looked toward the door. She didn't know what had just happened, but she could feel the air change. Feel his intensity level ratchet up.

"What's the difference between real whipped cream and that stuff in a tub?" he asked.

As distractions went, it was blatant and obvious. Jade debated for another second, then decided he was too much a cop to tell her anything he didn't want to.

"The difference? Mostly flavor."

"Yeah? I don't think I've ever had it before."

"So many things you haven't done," Jade teased. Then, wanting to lighten the mood, she scooped up a fingerful of the rich whipped cream and offered it to him. Dark eyes intent on hers, Diego hesitated. Since he was a smart man with a finely honed instinct for anything sexual, she knew that he knew exactly what she really wanted to offer, and it wasn't just rum-infused sugary goodness.

She held her breath. As soon as his mouth wrapped around her finger, though, the breath whooshed out. His lips were as soft as his tongue was hot.

Oh, God, it felt good. He slid his tongue along her finger, then sucked softly. Wet heat gathered between her thighs, making her want to squirm. His eyes locked on hers, he slowly, so deliciously slowly, released her. He didn't lean back, though. Instead, he gestured with his chin to the bowl.

"More."

Her eyes locked on his, Jade scooped up more whipped cream. But instead of lifting it to his mouth, she wiped it on her lower lip in invitation.

His eyes gleaming with passion, he leaned forward. His gaze held hers as he swiped his tongue over her lip.

"Mmm," he murmured. Then, as if he couldn't get enough, he sucked her lip into his mouth, nibbling gently.

Jade almost whimpered when he pulled away. "So…" she said slowly, smoothing her hands down his shoulders and over the warm expanse of his chest.

"So?"

She wet her lips, then met his eyes. She knew she probably looked nervous. Or maybe a little freaked out. But she also knew he had the power to see past that. To the desire. The passion. The intense need she had for him.

"Do you want to see more of my lingerie?" she blurted in a breathless rush. Asking for anything for herself was hard enough, but asking when they both knew it was a bad idea? Oh, man.

Diego's smile was slow, wicked and totally hot. The worry in her body melted away, along with most of her thoughts, all of her resistance and every objection she'd ever had. His hands tightened on her hips, pulling her closer, brushing against her.

The long, hard bulge in his jeans pressed against her belly. Jade's knees turned to Jell-O. Desire spiraled, tight and tempting, tightening her nipples and making her pulse race.

Her fingers dug into his chest. Not out of desire this time, but purely from a desperate attempt to keep from oozing into a lusty puddle on his feet.

"Can I ask one little favor?"

"Anything," she promised breathlessly.

"Will you wear those boots with your lingerie?"

NEVER ONE TO WAKE EASILY, Diego slowly worked his way out of the depths of sleep. His brain sputtered to a start. Then, like a beeping answering machine overflowing with urgent messages, he tuned in to his body.

It was wide-awake and horny.

With good reason. He sighed, reveling in the delighted exhaustion that only intense sex could bring.

He'd known she had a deep, intense sensual streak. A woman didn't wear the kind of lingerie she did and not enjoy sex.

And having tasted her before, he'd known the sex between them would be awesome. But last night? Diego threw his arm over his eyes to block the dim light that could only be the morning sun. Last night—and those boots—had been mind-boggling. His awareness might only be registering in the single digits, but he was 100 percent sure of two things.

That Jade was incredible.

And the two of them, together? Freaking awesome.

And nothing said good-morning better than a warm, sleepy round of freaking awesome.

"Mmm," he mumbled, not opening his eyes as he reached out to haul Jade—and her sleepy, sexy warmth—

much closer. He wanted to feel her naked flesh sliding beneath his again. To taste her as her cries of ecstasy filled the room.

Blinking groggily, his eyes automatically locked on Jade.

She was still fast asleep and wrapped in a very thin, very smooth sheet. Not as smooth as her skin, he decided as he skimmed his hand down her back, taking the fabric down as he went.

"Wake-up time," he murmured with a wicked grin. What a sight. Her hair surrounding her like strands of sunlight, Jade's face was buried in the ice-blue satin of her pillow. Which left him with the tempting view of her bare back. And, he noted as his body leaped ahead to fully awake, the sweet curves of her just-as-bare butt.

She had a tattoo. Right there where the curve of her butt sloped toward her spine, just above the left cheek. A tiny purple-and-gold butterfly, flying free from a vivid green cocoon. He lightly traced his index finger over the cocoon, noting that the artist had made the threads look like bars.

Is that how Jade saw herself? Trapped as she tried to change? There, at the edge of his consciousness, was her declaration of love. He'd tried to ignore it the night before. He tried to keep on ignoring it now. No point in desperately latching on to something that wasn't real. That couldn't be real. Better to focus on what he could depend on.

Like how delicious Jade was.

Giving in to his body's demand, he shifted down to press a kiss on the butterfly. Safe flight, he wished her with a grin. Because he intended to make it a wild one.

He slid his hand over the gentle slope of her butt, sliding between her thighs with whisper-soft fingers.

She stirred. Mumbled something, then burrowed her

face deeper in the pillow. The move angled her leg just a little. Just enough for his hand to find easy entry.

Diego's fingers tangled in the warm curls. Slid over the soft bud. Burrowed slowly, ever so slowly, into the welcoming depths.

She gave a low, mewling sort of noise into the pillow, her hips pressing against his questing fingers.

Diego shifted lower, nibbling a line of kisses up the firm, smooth skin where her thigh met her butt. Her perfect, butterfly-decorated butt. His fingers swirled, dipped, slid in and out. Her body, awakening much faster than she did, grew slick, wet. Welcoming.

His mouth watered. His dick, already rock-hard, pulsed against the silk sheet. With his unoccupied hand, he gently pressed her thighs apart, giving himself more access. And a better view as his fingers danced along the glistening pink flesh.

"Oh, my." Jade awoke with a throaty moan. He glanced up to see her grab the pillow, silk clenched tight in her hands. Her body trembled. Her thighs tensed.

He blew, his breath hot on her quivering flesh.

And sent her over the edge.

Her cries of delight filled his ears. Warmed his heart. And made his body ache.

Throbbing with desperation now, he grabbed a condom from the pile she kept next to the bed. Then he slid up her body, reveling in her moan of approval. Poised above her, he shifted his hand under her hips to raise her higher to meet his thrust.

He slid into the hot, slick heat of her with a groan.

Her moan was muffled by the pillow, her butt tight against his hips as she undulated, swirled. Tempted.

Diego almost lost it right then and there.

Carefully, slowly, he slid in and out of her tight flesh.

"Mmm," she moaned, her sigh long and welcoming.

He moved faster.

"Oh, Diego," she panted. Over, and over, and over. Her breath came in gasps now. Her words in pants. Her thighs quivered under his fingers.

Diego plunged harder.

Deeper.

She cried out.

Her body arched, stiff and shaking, against his.

He pressed deeper.

Swirled his hips.

Through slitted eyes, he saw her fingers clench the sheets, yanking the fabric toward her as if to keep herself from flying away as she cried out one more time.

It was probably the most erotic thing he'd ever seen.

Diego pulled back, his body so tight, so desperate for relief, that he had black spots dancing in front of his eyes.

He plunged.

She gave a mewling sound of satisfaction.

He groaned, then plunged again. Once. Twice.

Then he exploded. Stars echoed his release, flashing bright and intense behind his eyes.

His heart pounding so loud it sounded like a machine gun ricocheting through his head, Diego collapsed. Careful not to crush her, he slid to his side, pulling Jade's still-trembling body against his.

She was incredible.

Responsive. Enticing. Delicious.

She was everything he'd never known he wanted in a woman.

And everything his heart now swore it couldn't survive without.

As he tried to find his breath, and his sanity, Diego reveled in the warm softness of Jade's still-trembling curves.

He'd figure it out, he promised himself. Once the blood returned to his brain, he'd find a way to solve this mess his heart had made.

Suddenly there was a loud crash. Adrenaline surging, his body flew into a protective arch over hers. He made sure she was tucked safe under him even as his hand automatically flew to the small of his back. His naked back, since his gun was tucked in a drawer across the room.

Shattering glass exploded with a staccato tinkling. Something rough scraped wood, slid through glass. The cat gave an angry yowl, as if it'd been hit.

"Sophie!" Jade cried.

"Don't move!" Holding her tight, Diego waited. Jade wasn't having any of that, though. She struggled beneath him, trying to see past his body.

"Persephone."

As if she'd conjured the feline, as soon as the words left her mouth, four feet stabbed Diego in the back. He winced, but managed to hold back his manly yelp.

"She's fine," he muttered, cringing as the animal scampered for the safety of Jade's arms. Since that put the furry mass smack-dab between them, he figured—safe or not— it was time to move.

Slowly, his senses on full alert, he rolled off Jade, still careful to keep his body between her and the window.

"Shit."

"Oh, my…" She gave a horrified gasp against his back. "Why…"

She couldn't finish the sentences, clearly overcome by the sight of her window splattered in a million pieces across her bedroom. There, in the middle of shards and splintered wood, was a brick with the word BITCH written in fat black marker.

Diego wanted to hit something. Or, his gaze shot to the now-empty window frame, someone.

Swinging his feet off the bed, he'd just reached for his jeans when Jade grabbed his arm. "Be careful," she cautioned.

He shot her an amused look. "I don't think the brick is loaded."

"Of broken glass, silly. Watch your feet and shake out your clothes before you put them on."

He didn't know when—or if—he'd last been called silly. Or why it made him want to grin. Maybe it was Jade, her hair snarled like sunshine around her head, the terrified cat cuddled close to her chest. Her naked chest.

Wishing he could switch places with the yet-again growling and hissing cat, he gave his jeans a quick shake before pulling them on. The glass pattern swept clear under the bed, so he shook out his boots, then yanked them on, too.

Careful not to step on glass and damage the floor further, he walked over to examine the brick. Spying a piece of white fabric on the floor, he grabbed it to lift the object. Part of her curtain, he realized, keeping his face stoic, clear. No point upsetting her by letting her see the fury that was pounding through him.

Nope. He'd save that for the asshole who did this.

"You know who it was," Jade said, her eyes wide as she stared at his face. What? Could she really see into his soul? And why didn't that bother him more?

Diego just shrugged, though. He was on the job now, and he could see the end of the case as clearly as he could see her pretty face.

His entire career, his goal was to close the case as fast as possible. For the first time, he hated finding the answer.

"Are you going to arrest someone now?" she asked, setting the cat on the bed, then wrapping a sheet tight around her body. Diego looked around, then opened the closet to find a pair of hard-soled slippers to hand her.

"I have to go through channels. Talk to Applebaum, confirm a couple of things."

His jaw clenched. And deal with the fact that it was time to go.

MISERY WASHED OVER Jade with the same power as the orgasms that had pounded through her the night before. He was leaving. Sure, he had those channels to go through, the cop steps to take. But he was leaving.

She wanted to cry.

"Is it a bother, having to take those extra steps?" More important, did they take a lot of extra time? She hoped so.

"The trials of a guest cop," he said with a dismissive shrug.

She almost asked if he'd decided about the job offer. But that meant a) letting on that she knew about the offer. And b) pressuring him to make a decision not only about the job, but about them.

The idea of asking him, of hearing his answer, scared the hell out of her. Jade clutched the sheet between her fingers, wishing she was brave enough to ask. Strong enough to tell him that she wanted him to stay. But if he stayed, it'd be for her.

"I'll be right back. Gonna get the vacuum."

She opened her mouth to call him back. Then snapped it shut again when a wave of hot black terror washed over her at the prospect of confronting both her emotions and his decision. She couldn't leave. Not without hurting her family. And herself, she realized. She was a part of this town. Seeing it through his eyes had shown her that.

The only drawback to living in Diablo Glen was not having a career she loved. Well, a career, and Diego.

Even if she found the nerve to ask him to stay, she knew he'd choose to go. A guy didn't grow up exposed to the ugly side of small towns, then want to live in one.

Back, vacuum in one hand, grocery bag and paper towel in the other, he lifted the brick without touching it and settled it into the bag. Then, setting it aside, he stood with the vacuum cord in hand. He didn't plug it in, though.

"Applebaum mentioned a local job," he said finally, tonelessly. As if he had no opinion. As if he was filling her in on something he knew she already knew, and figured he should do the polite thing and mention it. "A cop deal, here in town. You probably heard about it."

Jade nodded. She swallowed hard, wishing she were brave enough, strong enough, to ask him to sacrifice for her. That he give up his big promotion and transfer, and stay here. To risk hearing that he didn't care enough to want to.

Besides, she'd already used him enough.

For excitement and great sex, sure.

But she'd hoped through him she'd find the answer to making her dreams come true.

Turned out, he was the answer.

But she couldn't ask him to give his up to make her happy.

"I did. But is that the kind of thing you'd want to do?" she heard herself saying as if from far, far away. "Be tied down to a small town? It'd probably be pretty boring compared to what you're used to. There aren't any promotions or juicy cases to solve around here. And who knows how long it'd take for another panty-thief caper to ensue."

She tried to smile at that last part, but her face felt stiff.

Painful. Almost as painful as the little pieces of her heart breaking away as she realized this was it.

He'd solved the case, so he was leaving.

She was too afraid to ask him not to.

And equally afraid of what would happen if he actually stayed.

14

A CHILLY DECEMBER AFTERNOON probably wasn't the best time to sit in the park. Still, Diego had needed time and space to think. He slumped on the bench and glared at the swings. What had he expected? For Jade to be excited when he'd mentioned the job here? To want him to stay? He'd barely got the words out before she'd rejected the idea. Clearly, he'd served his purpose, rocked the sex and had shown her a good time. But faced with the possibility of having him around on a long-term basis? She wasn't much interested.

Story of his life.

"There you are."

Frowning because he hadn't heard the approach, Diego inclined his head to Applebaum. "How'd you figure on finding me here?"

"Just followed the trail of bread crumbs. Or, you know, asked a few people if they'd seen you about."

The older man settled onto the bench and pulled out his pipe. Diego's glance slid to the no-smoking sign. Was he going to have to bust the mayor? Kinnison would love that.

But Applebaum didn't light the pipe. He just passed it from hand to hand. And waited.

The man would have made one hell of a torturer. He'd just sit there like a benevolent grandpa, waiting for his prisoner to blurt out everything and anything.

It was a trick Diego liked to use himself. Except for the grandpa part, of course. Still, it shouldn't work on him.

A few more minutes of forcing himself not to look toward Jade's house, not even to see if Persephone was still watching from the window, and Diego shifted. He stretched his shoulders. Cracked his neck. Ground his teeth. And finally, he sighed and gave in.

"The thefts never made sense," he said quietly, dropping his voice even though nobody was close enough to hear. "The nature of it suggests a sexual focus. There aren't too many other ways to regard the theft of women's underwear."

"Unless the thief is a closet cross-dresser too afraid to actually buy his own," Applebaum mused aloud, his attention focused on buffing the gleaming wood of his pipe.

Diego snorted. Then he slanted the other man a curious look. "And would there be suspects if that were the case?"

"There would. But given the sizes of underwear stolen, and the fact that I looked into this particular resident myself to make sure he really is in Florida visiting his daughter, I think we can rule that out."

"I'm oddly comforted to know you do have perverts," Diego murmured. Too bad it added another weight on the stay-in-Diablo-Glen side of the scale. Unable to resist a peek, he glanced toward Jade's. His lips twitched. Persephone had plastered herself, lengthwise, up the window as if she was trying to reach the ceiling.

Applebaum followed his gaze, smiling around the pipe now clenched between his teeth.

"You're on to something?"

Diego shrugged. "I know who did it. I just don't have that last puzzle piece. It feels big, though."

"The motivation for stealing panties is big?"

Diego laughed at the sarcasm in the older man's voice. Then he shook his head. "Like I said, it was set up to look sexually motivated. But it isn't. That's what threw me."

"You think you know what that missing piece is, don't you?"

Diego nodded.

"But?"

Diego almost blurted out all the reasons he didn't want to close the case.

That he'd grown attached to the town.

When he made this arrest, people were going to get hurt. People he'd come to care about.

An arrest meant saying goodbye.

And he was in love with Jade.

"No buts. I need to go over a few things with you first, though."

"Give me ten minutes to take care of a few details. I'll meet you at my office."

Without another word, no questions, no recriminations, no nagging insistence to share information, Applebaum sauntered away.

Leaving Diego alone, trying to find the courage to take the scariest leap of his life.

The leap of faith to believe that the feelings he had for Jade were not only real, but that they had a chance of lasting in the real world.

JADE ATTACKED THE STACKS in the far back corner of the library with a vengeance. As if eradicating every speck of dust on books that nobody ever checked out would clear her head, settle her stomach and help her figure out what the hell to do with herself now.

How sad was she. Little Ms. Empowerment, emotionally cowering behind dusty books. Because she wasn't brave enough to risk hurting anyone. Not herself. And definitely not anyone else. Not when it really mattered.

Maybe she should get a new tattoo. FRAUD in big fat letters.

"Hiding?"

"Working." Shoulders stiff, she didn't look at her sister. Just kept on dusting.

"C'mon out to the lobby."

"I said I'm working, Ruby."

"Beryl's out front. She's a mess."

Pulled out of her pout, Jade tossed the duster on the cart, wiped her hands on a cloth and faced her older sister. Bare-faced, wearing a ratty sweatshirt and jeans, Ruby looked stressed. But Ruby never looked stressed.

"What happened?" It had to be bad if she brought it to the library instead of waiting to deal with it at home, especially since their mother only put in a few hours doing paperwork on Sundays.

"She broke up with Neal."

"Oh." Jade tried to sort through the dozens of emotions to settle on a reaction. Relief was most prominent. And, she figured, the least welcome.

"Exactly."

The look on Ruby's face made it clear she wasn't on the Neal bandwagon either. Why hadn't Jade known that? Was she such a total wimp that she didn't even tell—or ask—the people she loved things just because she worried they'd have a different opinion?

She was finding out so much about herself this week-end. And other than her newly discovered ability to straddle a guy while wearing five-inch heels, none of the rest was very admirable.

"C'mon, Jade," Ruby prodded. "And remember, this is going to be hard for her. But be careful, because I don't know if it's a real breakup or just a tiff."

"I know how to be supportive," Jade snapped.

Together, they wove through the tall bookcases and display racks toward the lobby. As Ruby continued to whisper instructions on how to be a good sister, Jade pulled on her most sympathetic face. At the same time, she shoved her real opinion of Neal—quite likely colored by her feelings about his mother—into a dark corner of her mind.

The lobby was empty. Silent and dim.

The office door was closed, blinds pulled.

"How anticlimactic."

Ruby's lips twitched. "So we wait to be sympathetic and helpful."

Jade shrugged. It wasn't as if she had anywhere to go.

"I brought your purse. You left it at Mom's when you bailed on the party yesterday," Ruby said as they both stared at the closed office door. "Where'd you go? Rebecca Lee was looking everywhere for you. Then someone mentioned that they saw you leave with the hottie cop, so we figured you'd found other entertainment."

"What'd Rebecca want?" Jade didn't feel like justifying her departure. Sharing Marion's rudeness wouldn't help support Beryl, and outing their mother's make-out session was just, well, weird.

"I think she wanted you to do a styling party for Cathy's wedding. She's treating the bride and her sisters, as well as five of their friends, to a weekend in the city. She wanted to know what you'd charge to go along, help the bride choose the perfect trousseau and outfit the wedding party for all the bridal events. You know, rehearsal dinner, luncheons, bridesmaids' tea."

"That sounds really…cool," she decided. Cathy Lee and her sisters were pretty girls, all a little on the heavy side. They'd be so fun to style, to show them how to dress to make themselves feel great and look fabulous.

"I heard her talking to people about it at the party," Ruby continued. "It's a really hot idea. By the time they'd finished sandwiches and moved on to dessert, at least three other people were talking about contacting you. A couple more wanted to know prices so they could put you on their Christmas list."

Jade laughed in surprise. "Me? On a wish list? That's so wild."

"Is it something you'd be interested in?"

Jade leaned against the countertop and considered. It was a fun concept. Something she'd be good at and would enjoy. The trick would be finding the right clothes, since she didn't have a store or designer affiliation. But all that would take was a day or so of preshopping, maybe making a few new contacts and checking out store websites ahead of time.

If it actually made money, and the teaching took off, she could quit the library. Build up her contacts, put together a few styling events, maybe expand her online presence. She could actually call herself a stylist by occupation.

Excitement stirred.

Wouldn't that be too freaking awesome?

"I think it's definitely something I'd like to try," she finally said, trying to temper her excitement.

"What about wanting to leave? Wouldn't you rather focus on that?" Ruby asked quietly. "If you want to, we'll help. Berry and I were talking last night. We didn't realize how much we'd put on you here, or how trapped you might feel."

Trapped.

Jade looked at the closed office door and sighed. Was she trapped? Or was she just afraid? The possibility of building a career as a stylist here was so exciting. The cost of living was much lower than in a big city, especially since her house was paid for. She had support, friends and a solid foundation in Diablo Glen.

All she needed was a career she loved.

And Diego.

She pressed a shaky hand against her churning stomach. Could she ask him to stay? Ask someone to put her wants, her needs, ahead of their own dreams?

What if he resented it, as she had?

What if he didn't care enough to even give the idea a try and find out if he resented it?

She laid her head on the cool desk and sighed.

What if she was such a big wuss, she scared herself out of reaching for both her dream, and her dream man. The dream seemed to be finding its way back to her, whether she'd earned it or not.

The man, though? Once he roared out of town, she was sure he was gone for good.

"Are you okay?" Ruby asked, her hand warm and supportive as she rubbed Jade's shoulder. "You don't have to decide now, you know. We are here for you. And Mom will be, too. Although she's been acting a little funny lately. Have you noticed?"

Jade suddenly remembered the first shock yesterday, before seeing her thong flying from Santa's head.

The mayor. Kissing her mother.

Kissing.

She winced. Then, with a sigh, relaxed. Mayor Applebaum was a good guy. And Mom had been alone for a long time now. She deserved to be happy, to have a little fun. The question was, would Ruby and Beryl agree?

Before Jade could decide whether or not to share what she'd seen, the door opened. They both looked toward the front of the library. And winced.

"Damn," Ruby whispered.

Marion strode in with a rain cloud of a scowl, looking like the Grinch before he'd found his heart.

Jade grimaced. "I forgot she was coming in today."

"This is going to be ugly," Ruby predicted, setting her feet more firmly into the floor, as if preparing to go to battle to defend her little sister.

A good thing, too, because just as Marion was stomping her way down the steps toward Jade, the office door opened and out came Beryl and their mother.

"You," Marion barked, whirling to glare at the youngest Carson.

Before she could follow that up, the door opened again. Jade stepped forward, prepared to throw herself at the feet of whoever it was.

Diego.

Would she ever get used to how gorgeous he was?

Her heart thumped, then took off at the speed of sound. She'd rather throw herself on something besides his feet, but she'd take what she could get. And given that her mother was right there, and the mayor at Diego's shoulder, that was probably for the best.

"Gentlemen," she greeted in a bright tone. "What brings you in today? Can I interest you in a holiday book?"

"Actually, we're here to let you know we arrested the Panty Thief," Diego said.

"What? Who?" everyone asked at once.

"Neal Kroger," he said quietly. Instead of looking at

Jade, he stared at Neal's mother. Jade ripped her gaze from her sister's face, pale with shock, to look at Marion. The older woman looked furious. As if she wanted to leap across the room and tear a chunk out of Diego's flesh.

It was kind of scary.

"How dare you. What right do you have to come into our town and make such a baseless, ridiculous accusation?"

Diego didn't say a word. He just pulled out his badge and held it in front of her, offering up proof of where his rights came from.

"Why?" Jade asked her quietly. "What'd any of those women do to him? What was the point of stealing underwear?"

"Distraction," Diego said with a shrug. Then he gave her a small smile, just a little wicked around the edges. "He got the idea from your cat, by the way."

"That damn cat," Marion snarled. "This is all ridiculous. That cat's the one who stole the underwear. You caught it in the act, remember."

"Marion," the mayor said quietly, as if trying to get her to slow down and think before her next idiotic accusation. Since Jade was still smarting at the suggestion the older woman had made the previous day to put the cat down, she hoped Marion kept on babbling and digging her own grave.

"You have nothing on my son," the woman said, her furious tone echoed in the fist she shook at Diego. "Nothing, you hear me?"

"Actually, we have enough proof that the D.A. is doing backflips," Diego interrupted. "Right down to the brick he threw because he blamed Jade for Beryl dumping him. As to why? It was all a distraction."

Clueless, Jade shook her head. Everyone else looked just as confused. Everyone except the mayor, who looked resigned. And Marion, who just looked pissed.

Despite all the drama, the confusion, the fury on Marion's face, all Jade could think about was one thing.

Diego was making an arrest.

He was done here.

Her lower lip trembled. They were done now.

HIS BODY TENSE, Diego questioned his sanity. What had he been thinking, taking this route? He should have waited, got her when she came home. But he'd wanted to do this here, in front of Jade and her family. He'd wanted to make sure they had closure.

And yes, he'd wanted to show off a little. He figured seeing him do his job would either convince her that his being top cop in Diablo Glen was a great idea. Or it'd show them both that she couldn't handle his job. Either way, he had to know.

"This is all your fault," Marion Kroger spat at Beryl, glaring at the younger woman as if she'd like to take a go at her face. "First you broke my son's heart, now you're getting your sister's fancy city boyfriend to cause trouble for our family. I'll sue you, and your family, for libel. For slander. For pain and suffering."

Diego rolled his eyes.

"Mrs. Kroger, you might want to chill down. Quit bitching at Beryl," he said. "It's not her fault your son was an ass."

Okay, so that last part had been inappropriate. But it'd scored him a lot of points with the Carson women, if their grins were anything to go by. And a man making a major career move had to play to his future.

The old lady gave an outraged gasp. When it didn't elicit the sympathy she wanted, she gave a huff and slammed her arms over her chest.

"Rudeness is not acceptable. I'll be contacting your superior, young man."

"I'm sure he's been expecting a call or two," Diego said with a shrug. "You might not want to waste yours complaining about me, though. Better to use it to call your lawyer."

Her stance shifted from irate to nervous with the twitch of her pudgy fingers.

Diego slanted a glance at the mayor. His eyes sad, Applebaum gave a resolute nod of the head.

"Marion Kroger, you're under arrest." Diego followed the announcement with the charges, then the so-familiar-he-chanted-it-in-his-sleep Miranda. He wasn't positive she heard him, though, because she was yelling at Beryl, who was now hiding behind Ruby. Jade and Opal flanked the other women, making a united front of anger.

And he thought being a cop in a small town would have been so easy it'd be a bore? Despite the gravity of the situation, a grin escaped. To cover it, and to yank control back before this turned into a catfight, Diego stuck two fingers between his lips and whistled.

As one, the five women turned to stare at him, their faces painted with varying degrees of offended.

It was Applebaum who grinned this time.

"Excuse me," Diego said formally. "But I'm trying to make an arrest here."

"I thought you said Neal was stealing all those undies," Beryl said, her tone equal parts shock and horror.

"He was. He's also been arrested for assault and destruction of property."

"He's the one who threw the brick through my window?" Jade asked.

When her mom and sisters started peppering her with questions, Diego lifted his hand again. He didn't even get his fingers to his lips this time, though, before they quieted to hissing whispers.

"Yeah. Minor charges, compared to his mother's, but he's definitely going to do time."

Marion Kroger hadn't paid any attention to the charges because she'd been too busy playing drama queen, but this got her attention. Her face stiff, her gaze shifted from Diego's to the mayor's and back. Gauging what they knew, probably. Wondering how strong the charges might be.

"I'm innocent of any wrongdoing," she claimed.

"Human trafficking, harboring and hiring illegals, tax evasion are the initial charges," Diego told her. The gasps and whispers around the room echoed to emphasize the accusations.

The Kroger woman stared, stone-faced for a few seconds. Debating denial, Diego figured. It'd be harder to cop a plea deal if she confessed.

"I didn't do anything wrong." Her gaze shot from person to person, searching for something. Sympathy probably. When she didn't find it, she dropped her chin and gave a sniffle. "What makes you think you can get away with this?"

"It's pretty easy when we found proof at your house. A dozen illegal aliens you were hiding, and exploiting in your orchards. Transit records and bookkeeping ledgers recording the funds you were paid as part of the underground trafficking movement." Diego shrugged. "Sounds like you did plenty wrong to me."

"How dare you? Do you know who I am? What I do for this town?" The mayor shifted, just one foot to the other. But it was enough to put a cork in that line of outrage. She sucked in another breath.

Diego held up one hand for her to stop before she could get going again.

He'd had enough. They had the truth, it was time to end this. Besides, he had much more important things to do now. Like plan his life with Jade. He inclined his head toward the entrance. The mayor nodded, walked over and unlocked the heavy doors. When they swung open, the two immigration officers he'd contacted were standing there, ready to haul her off.

"It was the pressure," Kroger babbled as soon as she saw the uniforms. Her eyes widened, her face drooped. She gave a huge sigh and did everything but toss her wrist over her forehead. "The overwhelming emotional and mental pressure. It was so hard, raising a child alone. The expenses of keeping the orchard up, of surviving in this economy. I wasn't thinking clearly."

Diego gave an impressed nod. "That's pretty good. I don't think it'll get you an insanity plea. But it's a good foundation for emotional distress. You might want to work on the tears, though. It took Immigration Services seventeen evidence boxes and a bus to haul everything and everyone off your property. A little more drama might help balance that out."

Sandwiched between the two officers, the older woman glared. When one took her arm, she smacked him. "You keep your hands to yourself. Applebaum," she demanded, "you'd better come along. I want protection against police brutality."

"Not a problem." The mayor gave Diego a nod, letting him know he'd handle her from here. After giving Jade's mom's shoulder a quick squeeze, he followed Kroger and her escorts out the door.

The room was silent for a solid minute after their exit.

Diego waited.

Suddenly the women exploded. Questions, horror, exclamations. They flew faster than Santa's reindeer, ricocheting off the vaulted ceiling and bouncing from mother to daughter to sister.

There it was.

He leaned against the tall desk until they got past the initial shock. Jade got there first. Stepping away from the chattering horde, she gave him an intense, indecipherable look. He'd faced down junkies with loaded guns, but had the feeling she could hurt him a lot worse.

"Mom, can you take over my shift?" she said quietly.

The chatter stopped. Her sisters both gave him an appraising look while her mother focused exclusively on Jade. Apparently satisfied with what she saw on her daughter's face, Opal nodded.

Glancing his way, her eyes filled with too many emotions for him to read, Jade held out her hand and quietly asked, "Can we go for a walk? I need to talk with you."

This was it. His chance to convince her that she wanted him to stay around. To make her see that they had a future together. One she wanted to experience.

And if words didn't work, he still had his handcuffs.

15

JADE WAS GRATEFUL for the silence as they walked together into the park. She wished she could use it to gather her thoughts, to formulate how she was going to convince him to stay. But everything sounded stupid in her mind.

The gazebo lights were shining already, red and green glowing brightly against the white wood. She bypassed the Christmas display, heading for the playground instead.

"Swing?" she asked Diego as they reached the large metal structure. She waited until he sat, then took the swing next to his, sitting the opposite way so they faced each other.

And tried to find the perfect words to make her dreams come true.

"Wow. Big arrest" was all she could come up with, though. Jade wrinkled her nose. Talk about lame openings.

"You don't seem shocked."

"I'm not shocked," she mused out loud, smiling when he gave her a confused look. "I mean, I wouldn't have expected anything like this from the Krogers. Marion's always been such a stickler for her reputation, so focused on advancing her standing in the community. I wouldn't have thought she'd risk that."

"That's hardly a glowing character testimonial."

Jade grimaced. She didn't know which was worse. Harboring what she'd thought was an unjustified, unreasonable dislike for someone. Or being clueless that someone in her life was despicable enough to deal in human trafficking.

"You're right, it's not. I guess that's why I'm not shocked. There's always been something about her, and Neal, too, that bothered me. But I didn't know what it was. I mean, on the surface, they were nice people."

"Surfaces are deceptive."

"You saw through it, though," she said. "What was it that clued you in?"

"A lot of little things that when put together just added up. And one odd thing that really stood out."

"Like?" She really wanted to know how he'd figured it out. She'd lived in the same town as the Kroger family since she was a little girl. Her sister had almost married into the family. And other than a nagging something in the back of her head—which she'd easily ignored—she'd been clueless.

"Like Persephone."

"My cat?" Shocked, she glanced toward her house, a few yards away past the trees and hedges. "How?"

"She hated Neal. Not that she was overly friendly with anyone, but him? She growled, yowled and spit whenever he was around."

Confused, Jade nodded, but said, "But that's not exclusive to him. You saw it yourself. She did the same thing yesterday over my rescued underwear…"

Her words trailed off, her mouth forming an *oh*.

"I knew dogs could track things, find things through scent, but I didn't realize cats could."

"I didn't, either," he said. "But she reacted the same

way over your thong, and over that brick that was tossed through your window."

"So you arrested Neal?"

"So I used arresting Neal as an excuse to get onto their property and have a closer look."

"Because?"

He hesitated, then saying it quickly, like taking bad medicine, he said, "Intuition."

She wasn't sure what fascinated her more. That he believed in something so esoteric. Or how adorable his sheepish expression was.

"If I'd followed procedure, like my captain prefers, I'd have busted Neal and the case would be closed. But I knew there was something else going on. He'd hatched the panty thefts as a distraction because they had a busload of illegals coming in. But instead of moving them on out within a few days, Mrs. Kroger apparently saw a chance to bring in her harvest and not pay for labor."

"But if you'd followed procedure and arrested Neal here in town, you wouldn't have had anything to justify going out to the Kroger property," she confirmed.

"And by arresting him there, I had enough probable cause to call in Immigration." He grimaced. "Kinnison's still likely to bitch though."

"Will he mess up your promotion?" As much as she wanted him to stay, Jade didn't want it that way.

"Nah. I reported to Applebaum while on this job. He okayed the bust." Diego gave a wicked grin. "He gets credit for it, too. That's gonna piss Kinnison off even more."

"Probably not as much as it will losing such a talented detective to a big promotion," she said, reaching over to lay her hand on his knee. She pulled back after a second, though, needing to keep her wits about her for this next part.

"It's easy to see why you got the promotion. San Francisco will be lucky to have you on their force."

She watched his face, desperate to see a hint, any little bit of encouragement, to continue. He was in cop mode, though. Inscrutable and unreadable.

She swallowed hard before forcing the words past the lump of terror lodged in her throat. "Of course, Diablo Glen would be luckier to have you stay here."

His stoic expression flickered. Narrowing his eyes, he shifted backward on the swing to better see her face.

"I know you've got a lot to look forward to in San Francisco. It's a big promotion and a much more exciting place to fight crime than Diablo Glen." She bit her lip. Then, unable to hold back the words, unable to even imagine life without him, she blurted, "But I wish you'd stay here. Applebaum wants you to head up the new police department. Everyone's talking about it. And they all want you, too."

"What?"

Why did he sound surprised?

"Everyone loves you," she told him, stating the obvious. "At least, everyone I've heard mention the subject. They're all hoping you'll take the position."

She gave him a naughty smile, then added, "Of course, some of the ladies are hoping you'll take it because they think you add a sexy vibe to the view around town."

He pulled a face. Then he gave her another searching look. "What about you?"

She couldn't read his voice. Couldn't tell what he wanted to hear. So she had to go with what she had—the truth.

"I want you to stay. You'd be wonderful at the job. You're good for the town, and I think the town would be good for you." At his arch look, she put it all out there, reaching over to take his fingers in hers. "I want you to stay, for us. To see if we can make this work."

He didn't say anything. Jade's stomach pitched into her toes, but she continued anyway. "I have a lot more shoes. Boots. Sandals. The variety of lingerie and footwear combinations are endless."

His eyes turned to liquid heat and he gave a low hum of approval. Then he shifted, reaching over to lift her out of her swing and onto his lap.

Jade laughed in delight, wrapping her arms around his shoulders.

"If I hadn't already accepted the job, the shoe offer would have done it for me," Diego said with a laugh. Beneath the humor, though, his words held an emotion she couldn't read. Jade shifted, needing to see his face. In his eyes, she saw a joy that was almost childlike. So pure, so happy, it brought tears to her eyes.

"I was going to take it, move here and chase after you until you gave in," he told her. "I figured it'd take a few months, maybe some bribes, but I'd wear you down eventually."

"I can't believe you're really going to stay." Delighted, and feeling freer than she ever had, Jade snuggled deeper into his arms.

Strong, warm and so tight she didn't think he'd ever let her go.

Good.

His mouth took hers in a kiss so sweet, so gentle, her heart wept in delight. The feelings that poured through her, through them, were stronger than anything Jade had ever felt. Or ever dreamed of feeling. He was amazing. And he made her feel amazing.

"My hero," she whispered when he lifted his mouth. Needing a second, she buried her face in his throat, letting his scent fill her, empower her. She really, really did love him.

"What kind of bribes?" she asked when he released her mouth.

"I took the job on a probationary basis. Six months. I figured I'd have convinced you that you were crazy about me by then, and I could give you the option of us staying here." He pulled back so he could see her face, his eyes so intent they made Jade nervous. "Or, if it's what you wanted, I'd find a way to set things up here so you, so we, could move to San Francisco. Or Los Angeles, New York, anywhere you wanted."

Her heart turned into a puddle of gooey joy. Jade couldn't stop smiling. He was giving them a chance. A shot at a future together. Here, there, anywhere that made them happiest.

"Are you sure about this?" she asked. "You're giving up a promotion, aren't you?"

"I'm not giving up anything. I'm getting everything."

Diego reached out, his finger tracing the line of her jaw. Then, his eyes intent on hers, he leaned forward to brush his lips over hers in a soft promise of a kiss.

"Don't worry," he whispered.

Just like that, all Jade's fears melted away.

Right here, waiting patiently, was her every dream come true.

Jade giggled, the emotions exploding through her with the excitement of glitter and confetti. She threw her arms around Diego's neck.

"I love you," she declared happily.

"I've never had anyone love me. Never had anyone want me to stay around. You make me feel amazing." He pulled back, just enough to see her face. His eyes intent, his expression as serious as she'd ever seen it, he said, "I didn't believe it existed, to be honest. But you've made me believe that love is real. That I deserve it, and can give it. I love you, Jade. I never knew anything could feel this good."

"And it's only going to get better," she vowed, her words a promise to them both.

* * * * *

COMING NEXT MONTH FROM
HARLEQUIN® BLAZE™

Available December 18, 2012

#729 THE RISK-TAKER • *Uniformly Hot!*
by Kira Sinclair

Returned POW Gage Harper is no hero, and the last thing he wants is to relive his story. But can he resist when Hope Rawlings, the girl he could never have, is willing to do anything to get it?

#730 LYING IN BED • *The Wrong Bed*
by Jo Leigh

Right bed...wrong woman. When FBI agent Ryan Vail goes undercover at a ritzy resort to investigate a financial scam at an intimacy retreat for couples, he'll have to call on all his skills. Like pretending to be in love with his "wife" aka fellow agent—and almost one-night stand—Angie Wolf.

#731 HIS KIND OF TROUBLE • *The Berringers*
by Samantha Hunter

Bodyguard Chance Berringer must tame the feisty celebrity chef Ana Perez to protect her. Only, the heat between them is unstoppable and so may be the danger....

#732 ONE MORE KISS by Katherine Garbera

When a whirlwind Vegas courtship goes bust, Alysse Dresden realizes she has to pick up the pieces and move on. Now, years later, her ex insists he'll win her back! Alysse is reluctant, yet she can't deny Jay Cutler is the one man she's never forgotten.

#733 RELENTLESS SEDUCTION by Jillian Burns

A girls' weekend in New Orleans sounded like the breakout event Claire Brooks has been waiting for. But when her friend goes missing, Claire admits she needs the help of local Rafe Moreau, a mysterious loner. Rafe's raw sensuality tempts Claire like no other...and she can't say no!

#734 THE WEDDING FLING by Meg Maguire

Tabloid-shy actress Leigh Bailey has always avoided scandal. But she's bound to make the front page when she escapes on a tropical honeymoon getaway—without her groom! Lucky her hunky pilot Will Burgess is there to make sure she doesn't get too lonely....,

---

YOU CAN FIND MORE INFORMATION ON UPCOMING HARLEQUIN© TITLES, FREE EXCERPTS AND MORE AT WWW.HARLEQUIN.COM.

HBCNM1212

REQUEST YOUR FREE BOOKS!
2 FREE NOVELS PLUS 2 FREE GIFTS!

red-hot reads!

YES! Please send me 2 FREE Harlequin® Blaze™ novels and my 2 FREE gifts (gifts are worth about $10). After receiving them, if I don't wish to receive any more books, I can return the shipping statement marked "cancel." If I don't cancel, I will receive 6 brand-new novels every month and be billed just $4.49 per book in the U.S. or $4.96 per book in Canada. That's a saving of at least 14% off the cover price. It's quite a bargain. Shipping and handling is just 50¢ per book in the U.S. and 75¢ per book in Canada.* I understand that accepting the 2 free books and gifts places me under no obligation to buy anything. I can always return a shipment and cancel at any time. Even if I never buy another book, the two free books and gifts are mine to keep forever.

151/351 HDN FEQE

Name	(PLEASE PRINT)

Address	Apt. #

City	State/Prov.	Zip/Postal Code

Signature (if under 18, a parent or guardian must sign)

Mail to the **Reader Service:**
IN U.S.A.: P.O. Box 1867, Buffalo, NY 14240-1867
IN CANADA: P.O. Box 609, Fort Erie, Ontario L2A 5X3

Not valid for current subscribers to Harlequin Blaze books.

Want to try two free books from another line?
Call 1-800-873-8635 or visit www.ReaderService.com.

* Terms and prices subject to change without notice. Prices do not include applicable taxes. Sales tax applicable in N.Y. Canadian residents will be charged applicable taxes. Offer not valid in Quebec. This offer is limited to one order per household. All orders subject to credit approval. Credit or debit balances in a customer's account(s) may be offset by any other outstanding balance owed by or to the customer. Please allow 4 to 6 weeks for delivery. Offer available while quantities last.

Your Privacy—The Reader Service is committed to protecting your privacy. Our Privacy Policy is available online at www.ReaderService.com or upon request from the Reader Service.

We make a portion of our mailing list available to reputable third parties that offer products we believe may interest you. If you prefer that we not exchange your name with third parties, or if you wish to clarify or modify your communication preferences, please visit us at www.ReaderService.com/consumerschoice or write to us at Reader Service Preference Service, P.O. Box 9062, Buffalo, NY 14269. Include your complete name and address.

Bestselling Blaze author Jo Leigh
delivers a sizzling *The Wrong Bed* story with

Lying in Bed

Ryan woke to the bed dipping. For a few seconds, his adrenaline spiked until he remembered where he was. He groaned at the bright red numbers on the clock. "One a.m.? What…?"

The rest of the question got lost in the dark, but it didn't matter, because Jeannie didn't answer. His fellow agent on this sting must be exhausted after arriving late. "You okay?"

She tugged sharply on the covers, pulling more of them to her side of the bed.

Ryan could just make out her head on the pillow, her back to him, hunched and tight. Must have gotten stuck at the airport….

He curled onto his side, hoping to find the dream she'd interrupted. It had been nice. Smelled nice. He sighed as he let himself slip deeper and deeper into sleep…. The scent came back, a little like the beach and jasmine, low-key and sexy—

His eyes flew open. His heart thudded as his pulse raced. No need to panic. That was Jeannie next to him. Who else would it be?

Undercover jitters. It happened. Not to him, but he'd heard tales. Moving slowly, Ryan twisted until he could see his bed partner.

He swallowed as his gaze went to the back of Jeannie's head. Was it the moonlight? Jeannie's blond hair looked darker. And

HBEXP1212JLREV

longer. He moved closer, took a deep breath.

"What the—" Ryan sat up so fast the whole bed shook. His hand flailed in his search for the light switch.

It wasn't Jeannie next to him. Jeannie smelled like baby powder and bananas. The woman next to him smelled exactly like…

She groaned, and as she turned over, he whispered, "No, no, no, no."

Special Agent Angie Wolf glared back at him with red-rimmed eyes.

"Jeannie is being held over in court," she snapped. "I'd rather not be here, but we don't have much choice if we want to salvage the operation."

She punched the pillow, looked once more in his direction and said, "Oh, and if you wake me before eight, I'll kill you with my bare hands," then pulled the covers over her head.

No way could Ryan pretend to be married to Angie Wolf. This operation was possible because Jeannie and he were buddies. Hell, he was pals with her husband and played with her kids.

Angie Wolf was another story. She was hot, for one thing. Hot as in smokin' hot. Tall, curvy and those legs…

God, just a few hours ago, he'd been laughing about the Intimate at Last brochure. Body work. Couples massages. *Delightful homeplay assignments.* How was this supposed to work now?

Ryan stared into the darkness. Angie Wolf was going to be his wife. For a week. Holy hell.

Pick up LYING IN BED by Jo Leigh.
On sale December 18, 2012, from Harlequin Blaze.